The Airline Bullet
A Science Fiction Fantasy Tale
By Steve Presley

All characters and places described in this tale were fictitious. No living human
alive or passed away was characterized. Although cities and places were mentioned, no attempt was made to
accurately describe them. This was a work of pure fiction.

As a child, my mother read to me. I enjoyed that. All of my life I have liked literature. Sometime ago, I decided to
contribute to it and publish my own works. So here I created another tale for people to enjoy.

Writers create readings for people. This takes lengthy thinking, writing, and editing. Writers have minds that may
think up side thoughts, dead end phrases, characters, settings, and plots that do not go with their current project's
objective. This is waste. There always is some waste. It is a mystery to me that I can not explain from where and
why any material at all is ever created.

Teachers, intellectuals, students, and casual users of literature want something in their hands to read. A tangible is
highly desirable. It is mere entertainment. That is exactly what this current work is. Entertainment.

A piece of paper is blank. Something must be put there to be read. The writer does this.

Igears and idears
Gadgets, gizmotchies, contrivances, and appurtenances

Composition
Vocabulary
Spelling
Word choice
Grammar
Punctuation
Sentence construction

Theme building
Outline
Titles
Chapter organization
Character creation and use
Plot formation, development, and conclusion
Descriptive flourishes
Author's style
Linguistic skill

Curves and straights
Up and down
Left and right
Slants
Become symbols
Letters and numbers
Form words
Language
Thoughts
Sentences
Lines

Paragraphs
Chapters
Feelings, thoughts, settings, stories
Plans, organization
Book
There is nothing larger than one book
Literature

Writers want to produce lengthy literary masterpieces that are popular and dazzle their audience.

Creative writing is an art that takes skill to produce.
It can not be trained or taught.
The ability is innate.
Either you have it
Or you do not.

This is a Steam Punk Scientific Fiction Novel
Alternate titles: The Bullet, The Air Line, The Flyway, The Rail Cloud, The Sky Rail,
The Air Rail
---Time line--- 1889 England

Man makes things. He has to. He uses his hands and machines to make things that he needs. Man is skillful at this. He spends time and puts much work in making useful, sometimes complicated and elaborate things. Man is a creator. He has factories. These are buildings with machines that build things for sale. Man makes money building and selling things.

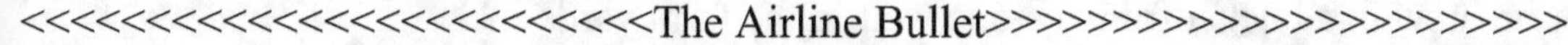
<<<<<<<<<<<<<<<<<<<<<<<<<<<The Airline Bullet>>>>>>>>>>>>>>>>>>>>>>>>>

Chapter 1. The Plowman

April 3, 1889, England. A country dirt back road led ahead. Here a thick woods covered the land on both sides. A brown thrush flew across the roadway. He disappeared into the shady darkness between the leafy trees. The afternoon sunlight shown down on the soil of the road. The harsh cold air temperatures were giving way to balmy warmer days. The frigid grip of winter was loosening to milder conditions. The gloomy days were gone. The winter chill was leaving as springtime warmth was gaining over the land. Snows had melted weeks ago leaving extra moisture in the soil. Trees were just putting out leaves. The dormant brown grass was now becoming green. Wild flowers were opening their blossoms with a burst of rich fresh color. Song birds had returned from their winter migration. The blue sky has several puffy white clouds moving slowly overhead. In the distance small hills crowned the horizon. Eventually the dense woods gave way to open meadows with flocks of white sheep grazing on the thick green grass. Cattle and horses herded about as well. Farm fields came into view. To the left a coursing creek turned to lie beside the road. For about eight miles it stayed there. Passing under the road through a rock bridge, the creek came to lay at the right side of the road.

A field appeared with a man walking behind a plow pulled by one brown horse. He was three quarters of the way done turning the soil. Wheat was to soon be sown here. The plowman slapped the reins and spoke to the horse directing the direction and depth of the new furrow. The gray clay soil was pulled up by the blade. It was fresh, wet, and darker than the unturned earth. The man had dirt on his black leather boots and on his lower pants legs. He walked in uneven steps stumbling on the uneven earth as the horse jerked him forward pulling the trace chains to pull the single tree and the plow along. The afternoon wore on. The shadows from the nearby trees beyond the field grew longer. Eventually the entire field was plowed. The man unhitched the plow leaving it on an edge of the field. The spring planting was now done.

The plowman walked behind the horse leading him along a path to a wooden barn with a shingle roof about a mile away. He unhitched the harness and bridle from the horse. He groomed the animal well and picked its hooves. The horse was put in a large stall. The man pitch forked a pile of hay into the stall from a large pile at one end of the barn. Several wooden buckets of water were carried from an outside well to a wooden trough at the stall's side. The man put a bag of oats in the bucket and lowered it past the slats of the stall gate to the dirt floor. The horse ate some hay, drank water, and moved over to the bucket with oats in it. Eagerly he ate all of the oats. Some oats were dropped from his black lips to the soil on the barn floor. The horse looked at the man with warm eyes. He tended to the other livestock as need be.

The man turned and walked out of the barn door and along a dirt path that led to a crude small stone farm house with a thatched roof. A group of red chickens walked beside him as he moved from the barn to the house. The man owned the small farm. He was a planter. He grew kitchen vegetables, feed crops, fodder, and seed crops. There was a small house, a barn, a shed, a chicken house, and a hog house. Sheep, chickens, hogs, beef cows, a few milk cows, and several horses lived there. The man wore coarse woolen clothes and worn leather plow boots. Sweat streaked his face where field dirt had accumulated. The farm was driven by meager means.

The man passed a shabby wooden slab shack. The weathered farmer went in an open doorway. From a pile on the ground, he picked up an armful of potatoes. A small gray mouse ran across the dirt floor. It ran into a burrow hole to disappear to safety. On a wooden shelf he picked one turnip out of a cloth sack. The turnip and potatoes were harvested last year.

The middle aged man with a work worn body walked back to the path towards the farmhouse. Passing the back door, he entered the kitchen. He washed the potatoes in a wooden washtub on the floor that was full of water. He loaded them into a pot with water. He built a fire in a fireplace building it up with kindling and logs. He cooked the potatoes until they were soft and ate several with some salt. Pealing the turnip, he sliced it and ate the entire thing raw. He drank cold water he drew in a bucket from a stone well in the farm yard.

This man wore a tweed brown woolen jacket and pants. The man had a tan cotton shirt under that. He had a brown felt brimmed hat over his thick brown hair. He was sweaty and dusty from plowing with the horse. It was getting dark. He found an oil lamp and lit it to beam brightness into the night.

This man was Chester Whittaker. At six feet one inch tall he weighed about 230 pounds. He had straight brown hair and moustache. This hair was parted on the left side. His body was strong and healthy for his forty-five years of life.

He found a cigar butt on the edge of the wooden mantle above the stone fireplace. He chewed on it for about a minute. The farmer positioned himself by the fire. Five logs were added to the flame to build it. The early night seemed cold even for early spring. The fireplace heat made his flesh hot. The back of his body was cold. Getting a burning stick from the fire, he lit the cigar. In a short time he had it smoking. The rich taste of tobacco came into his mouth refreshing him. He felt suddenly tired from a day's work. He sat in a stiff wooden chair beside the table. Chester rested heavily in the chair. Watching the fire, his mind went off into a thoughtless trance. After a bit, undressing, he washed his body at a basin on the kitchen counter with a cloth and bar of soap. He dried with a towel and put a blue robe over his flesh. With the lamp in his hand, walking along a short hall, found the single bed, turned back the covers, lay down, and recovered his body. The light flickered in the small room. He watched the ceiling for about thirty minutes. Leaning over to the lamp on a small bedside table, he blew it out and passed out into a deep night's sleep.

He awoke the next morning to the crow of a rooster. Standing in the cool quiet room, Chester looked out a window at the yellow orange sun just at dawn.

"A new day!" he thought to himself.

He dressed, shaved, tended to the animals, and collected three eggs, which he cooked for breakfast that was washed down with hot black coffee. He hitched a gray mare to a black buggy and rode away from the farm to the country dirt back road. After about ten miles Chester came to a small farm town. He put the buggy into a livery stable. Walking a stone path, he came to a train depot. Buying a ticket, he sat in a waiting room for twenty minutes. The air was still and silent for twenty minutes. Then a mechanical rumbling sound disturbed the quiet. It grew steadily in volume. A steam train came in to stop alongside the station. Several people dressed for travel with hand luggage got off the train. Chester and about four other persons boarded the train. It blew a whistle, emitted steam from both side cylinder petcocks, and slowly went up the track to the distance. The linkages moved, the wheels turned and the train chugged along the track making flat earth pass underneath it. On and on it went across wide stretches of the country side. After a good spell, the train entered a large industrial city.

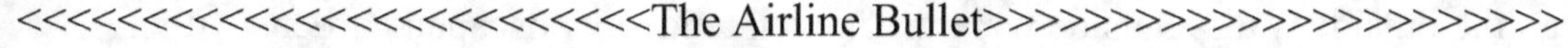

Chapter 2. Industry

Chester Whittaker was a self-made industrialist wealthy man. He ran several factories. He lived in a large three story Georgian mansion, with landscaped gardens, greenhouse, wine vineyard, reflecting pool, columned round temple to Apollo. The family was his wife Rosemary (Rose), four daughters, Mary Angelica, Vivian Victoria, Carrie Anne, and Sylvia Pauline.

Chester made his home in Solihull which was in the west midlands of central England on the Blythe River. This was in the region that Birmingham was located. It had a large residential area. He owned a beautiful wooden steam powered speedboat that he rode up and down the river. It had three props and a luxury cabin.

Chester was the son of a farmer. Chester quit school at grade six when he was twelve years old to work on his father's farm. He learned to read, write, tell time, manners, and do simple math. He is intelligent but did not complete his basic schooling. His is a life of work and not fancy ideas from teachers working in books.

Chester's parents and grandparents were farmers in Sussex. He spent time as a boy on four of the family's farms doing chores, taking care of livestock, doing field work, repairing equipment and buildings, plowing, planting and harvesting crops. He stayed in those farmhouses and ate freshly grown farm food. He hunted and fished with his father, grandfathers and uncles. The farmers he came from were happy people that knew little else about the world except farming. They did not read or write too well. The farms, crops, livestock, and families were what they had. This made them happy and they lived good lives. Chester's childhood was a happy one living with relatives on farms, changing seasons, holiday celebrations, and doing many things that he enjoyed with his cousins.

Chester appreciated everything that the world had to offer. He was capable of seeking his own version of happiness. He believed in God and so attended Saint George's Anglican Church. Chester thought prayer gave him strength in his life as the Holy Ghost loved him. He wanted to be a good person generating good will, living for duty and humanity. Reading the Holy Bible made his faith stronger.

The farm he labored on had been his father's. He was raised there by meager means. He watched his father toil and sweat by hard honest labor to support his family. Chester had worked there as he grew old enough. He liked that place in the country. It made him feel like he was a fundamental part of nature as his living came out of the soil. His father and mother matured and were sent off to heaven. Chester bought it and continued to work there. He had three brothers and two sisters. One brother was John Herbert. He was a house builder who lived in Essex (Exeter). He built sturdy dwellings. He paid his workers fair wages and treated them decently. He had the respect of all those that knew him. He had a son and a daughter. Another brother was Jack Earl. He lived in Nottingham. He owned a large lumber and saw mill operation. He had added a feed mill business. He married a divorced woman with two daughters and had another three daughters by her. The third brother was Peter Gordon. He was a ship builder in Liverpool. He had two sons and a daughter. One sister was Mary Alice. Living in west London, she had married a furniture manufacturer and had two daughters. Her husband made very high quality and expensive furniture. Rebecca Elizabeth was the other sister who was a school teacher at an Anglican academy in Newcastle. Married to a labor lawyer she had two sons.

Chester's wife, Rosemary (Rose), played a mahogany grand piano in a large sunlit parlor to one side of the house. Her lips had rouge and deep red lipstick. She wore a fluffy white dress of lace. A garnet broach was attached to her blouse. There was a large white lace rose on her belly. Two white lace ribbons were tied in her hair in neat bows. She wore white cotton stockings with black leather lace-up shoes. She had the scent of expensive floral daisy nectar perfume. Her hair was tied up on the top oh her head. On her hands were white lacy cotton gloves. She read a classical music books to select the proper keys to make the lovely melody that flooded up into the otherwise still and quiet air. There was an ornate cut crystal chandelier above the piano. Four gas lights flickered on low flames. Large windows made up the outside wall. Outside were green well tended landscaped gardens with a reflecting pool. Marble statues of classical Greek subjects stood on pedestals here and there. Carefully trimmed hedges lined off cement walkways. Several wood and steel benches provided places to rest. Black wrought iron fence-work provided another lattice. A wide winding staircase lifted up from the large living room to the second floor balcony. There were eight bedrooms, three bathrooms, a porch with a scenic view, and a den-library-smoking room. The second floor porch was recessed in the house walls out of direct sunlight. It looked down upon the lawn providing a generous view. A large bay window gave a view to the dining room adjoining the living room. A banquet table stood in room center. Six china cabinets, four linen chests, three beverage dispensers, and three hand operated ceiling fans were accessory to the table. There was a large front porch that wrapped around the two sides of the brick mansion. Wicker chairs and tables provided lounging comfort there. Roll down reed shades gave temporary and needed shade from the bright sun. Lilac shrubs grew at the porch edge. Ivy clung to the brickwork all about the house giving it a more tranquil atmosphere. As a young woman, Rosemary met Chester casually at a church dinner one Christmas eve. She had at that time been taken with him as a man with romantic possibilities for her future life. She presented herself to him enticing him to suit her emotionally if he so had the appetite. He seized the opportunity and became continually socially attached to her. After a year of courtship he married her. His life was built around Rosemary. She gave him a family and remained faithful to him as his wife. Rose gave him a wide social base to operate his life in. She graciously hosted many people who visited at their home, both friends and businessmen.

Sundays they rode an enclosed carriage pulled by two horses to church services. His family frequently went with them. The carriage was painted yellow with red striping lines to set off the plain spaces with some tasteful color. The English carriage horses were dark chocolate colored. The driver held the reins to keep the horses' heads down. They wore a brown leather harness and each had a black feathered plume on the top of the bridle. They lifted and dropped hooves in a well coordinated manner. It was a beautiful thing to watch. The carriage went along the dirt roadway. Hedges, houses, trees and side roads went past. Coming finally to the church yard, the carriage came to stop near the two large front doors. The couple opened the door, descended, and walked up the steps to pass out of sight through the doors.

Chester Whittaker's home was large grand, stately, and old. It was made mostly of gray granite. It was impressive but had a serious and dark personality. The house was very a large and a massive structure built on a formerly densely wooded hillside. The dwelling was a slate sheathed gothic with four towers. The windows were pointed cathedral structures with steel frames. The home while attractive had threatening overtones with a dimension of gloom suggesting secret chambers in its turrets peopled with ghostly beings from some far away place of horror. It was home for him, his wife, and children. He was an established man of means. This wealth was obvious when looking at the heavy scope of his house, grounds, and outbuildings.

Chester sat one evening alone at home. He was sitting in a large loggia with tall windows looking out on the wooded lawn and forest beyond. The windows were two stories tall. It was a mostly cloudy day without blue sky and direct sunlight. There was light but coming through the clouds it was indirect and diffuse. It was a milk white sky. He sat in a large padded chair. The chair was made of a frame of hardwood that looked like a lattice frame from the middle Ages. There was sufficient cloth and bedding material in it to make it a most comfortable place to rest sitting. He sat sipping hot tea with cream and brown sugar. There was a plate of sugary cookies and butter on a table beside the chair. Chester was at home. He was away from the daily responsibilities of his work week's schedule. This was not his work time or place. So he was at rest. He looked outside for a time and napped dozing off to semi-consciousness. His mind went anywhere that it wanted. He did not command it to go in any focused direction. There were paintings hung about upon the walls. Marble sculpture pieces stood about on the floor on stands of granite. Arabian and Asian rugs covered parts of the floor. Elsewhere it was polished oak. Fine woven tapestries hung down covering the walls. The dimmed sunlight washed into the room all about him from the windows. All was quiet except for his soft breathing and the periodic tinkling of the china as he consumed his refreshments. He thought in turn about his life, business ventures, his wife, family, his house, the land about it, his country, and the entire world. No he had not seen too very much of it. He knew that it was still there anyway. Still he thought of the world as a great large place and the starry skies beyond.

This was England in 1889. Chester owned livestock, mines, lumber, an accounting firm, stores, field crops, gem mining outfits in Africa, cargo sailing and trading ships, home building companies, a publishing house, a charity home for poor children, supported a hospital, and an engineering company. He possessed a steel business, Crown Steel. He built weapons, tools, steel bridges, sailboats, buggies, carriages, and wagons. He rode steam trains and county coaches. Chester owned a whiskey brewery, the Chester Oates Whittaker Brewery in Glasgow, Scotland and a chain of pubs to sell it. He was an inventor. 1889 England was mostly farming but factories and manufacturing was growing as the machine industrial age was here. Chester had interests in Glasgow, Coventry, Birmingham, London, Newcastle, and Cardiff. He owned sheep, the woolen industry, cotton farms, and textile mills. Mr. Whittaker started trading cows as a young man of fifteen years old. He traded up and made a fortune from wise dealings. Chester held numerous stocks, bonds, and large sums of cash piled up in dozens of English banks. He was a hard working money man. A capitalist.

He had created financial business, management firms that he met with regularly to steer all of his businesses and industries. He presented to his executives economic studies of trends, the cost of raw materials, labor, insurance, utilities, and the building expenses. He the calculated the cost of goods sold. He reported sales figures. Subtracting the expenses from the gross profits he discussed the margin of profit achieved. Expressing ways of gaining on these figures, he managed his holding toward more efficient returns for what he was investing in it. He realigned businesses for a better economy of effort. He planned the work so labor, time, materials, and money were lost at a minimum. Economize and optimize. Do the job intelligently. Do not be careless. Measure ten thousand times. Cut only once. He hated waste and poor planning. Being practical minded, he was able to run things very well. Profit was the driver of production. The supply chain, demand, return on investment, shipping expenses, and current buying trends were all factors. Business cycles were always present. He wanted to make what the people wanted. Chester visited each factory, walked about, talked to the people there, and kept up with what was going on.

Mr. Daniel Jeremiah Skokie was one of Chester Whittaker's superintendents. He traveled all of Chester's businesses, returned to Chester, made reports, and they decided what should be done on this or that to guide the businesses along. Mr. Skokie was a husky man of about 310 pounds and black headed. Hears of reading business figures had made him nearsighted so he wore silver spectacles.

Chester went fly fishing at a stream near a red waterwheel powered country mill. The surface of the water bobbed up and down in sheets of waves. This was elastic. The water was flexible like a watch spring or locomotive steam. It moved a bobber on his fishing line about in the water. The waves lifted this weight making it travel. It provided motion. A steel spring possibly could do this likewise. The bobber seemed to move in the water as the stream's waters raced past it. He dreamed of traveling long distances on a ship around the world. He watched the tree trunks, branches, and limbs sway in the breeze. The motion resembled a pendulum because they moved back and forth steadily. No, the tree was not an accurate time keeper. No, it did not move anywhere over the ground. The trunk had large roots keeping it stationary in the soil. Still the trees were wood. They had a unique kind of natural motion that was powered by the wind. The wind came from large volumes of air being heated differently. Cold air was thicker and heavier. It pushed into thinner and lighter warmer air. This made the air move as wind. The sun heated all the earth. All the power on earth, all the energy on the earth, and all the matter on the earth came from the sun. The sun, wind, and tree were a kind of a machine that moved. Sailboats moved. Wind pushed cloth sails on wooden ships over the water. Windmills also were a wind vehicle. Different kinds of energy caused forces that created motion. Chester dreamed of traveling above the trees in the air. The wind was in motion. Somehow he thought he may build a craft that traveled up above the treetops in the winds. They had power like the water in the river did. But how would he build such a flying device. His mind wandered on with this in silence. Near where he was fishing on a riverbank, horse pulled wagon moved along a roadway. The wagon was loaded with fairly large oak barrels. Chester thought that barrel shape was similar to a bullet. Maybe he could build a large bullet like oak barrel shaped people carrying contrivance that flew above the earth safely. His mind continued working on this as he fished. He was successful and caught six trout. Fishing was just pure luck.

Chester liked people and spoke as well and got along well with everyone. He was a sensitive man with feelings for how people were to be treated. He was a well liked and respected man. He loved his wife and daughters. The people who worked for him found him eager to be approached and dealt with.

Chapter 3. A Daydream Idea

Chester Whittaker liked to build things. He worked well with his hands using tools. He had built a few houses, furniture, several boats, and wagons. He liked transportation devices. In his mind he had concocted a new idea for a different kind of these. Once when hunting, he had daydreamed about bullets shape and how they travel from a gun through the air. Here was a machine, a gun, that propelled an object, shot shells and bullet slugs, rapidly through the air. Why not make a traveling machine like a bullet that people may get into and fly through the air to a new destination? This would not move over the ground on legs and wheels, up and down the land and turn this way and that. It would be up in the air, free of the earth, and travel like the wind. Yes, Chester pondered, there might be a new flying bullet carriage that he could make and use.

Chester wanted the bullet to be made well and perform good so as to be an inventive masterpiece. He drew on paper some images of a track that it was launched from the bullet itself, and other parts of machinery, and details like seating for people in the bullet, how it was launched, steered, and landed, boarded and exited by people. He had a large landscape oil painting of the bullet and track done by a local London artist.

A foundry forge in Cornwall, owned by Chester, made the best English carbon steel in the land. This was named the Alexander T. Swain Ltd. Steel Company. This was to be used to make the bullet. In Birmingham the James William Haycock Metal Company would make the brass, bronze, copper, tin, cast iron, lead and other metals needed. Some bushings were made of bronze and lead. Gears were to be made out of bronze, brass, steel, or cast iron. As different sizes and diameters were needed at different places in the machinery, different metals were to be used for the different gears. Some oak, spruce and ash woods were to be used. In Glasgow, Scotland his whiskey company, an agent of his, Cecil James Williams, obtained the oak and other woods needed, were taken from a Scottish forest was to be used to make the bullet's outer wooden barrel hull. The oak usually was used to make whiskey casks. Chester bought the Frederick D. Mason Clock and Watch Company in Newcastle. It would build the needed works.

Back in a large brick factory building, men were busy making parts for the bullet. A row of windows on the side walls let in the daylight. The floor was a polished oak. Large and small machines were busy. Belts, gears, shafts, drills, grinders, hobs, presses, planers, and stamping equipment made a rough roaring sound as they hummed along. Oscar Hadley, a workman, sat at his stool by a wooden workbench next to an outside wall. He was laboring machining gears for the bullet. He adjusted knobs and levers to guide the tooling to cut teeth in a gear blank's outer circumference.

Oscar said to Willie Dawson, another worker nearby, "I think that this idea of Chester's is a good one. He is an honest and practical man. If we all do our work well, these parts will fit together like they are supposed to. Then when it is turned on, it will do what will be expected. Willie, you mind what you are doing there and do it well. We all like Chester and owe him a good day's work for the money he is paying us."

Willie was filing the edge of a curved gear blank to debur it after a preliminary machining step. The work piece was tightly held in a vice attached to the edge of his wooden work bench. Willie stopped filing and looked up to hold Oscar's eyes as he replied, "Oscar, I always try to do my best here at work. But if you insist, I will be powerful extra careful here on this bullet work."

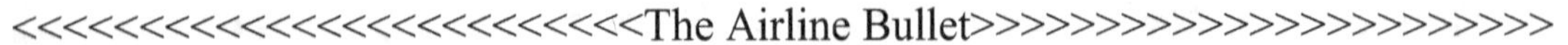

<<<<<<<<<<<<<<<<<<<<<<<<<<<<The Airline Bullet>>>>>>>>>>>>>>>>>>>>>>>>>>>>>

Chapter 4. Clockwork

One day Chester was watching carriages passing by his office in town. It was 4:00 P.M. It was afternoon tea time. Chester brewed his own tea. He in a tin pot he heated water with a kerosene flame, put loose tea in a tea tin with holes in it, and put this in the hot water. Later he added sugar and fresh cream. Chester held a tea saucer and a tea cup with a red and pink floral pattern on them. The tea was flavorful and stimulated him from a mild state of fatigue. He liked to daydream. Distance in miles was traveled. This took time. Distance traveled over a time was velocity. A distance changed with respect to time squared was acceleration or changing speed. It could increase or decrease (deceleration). A distance traveled with respect to time cubed was a jerk. This was a changing acceleration. Animals and people moved. Horses and wagons moved. Ships and steam trains also moved. Birds flew. All of these had motion, speed, acceleration, and change of position as well as direction. Why not come up with a new novel machine for traveling!

He drew up several wheeled wagons trying to create a new device. He worked and pondered two weeks doing this getting nowhere. At first the power for the bullet cart to be launched on the ramped track was to be horses and then maybe gunpowder using a large cannon. Horses were not strong or fast enough. Gunpowder was tool dangerous. Then steam power was considered. It had power. That was true. But it was so heavy that a steam engine could not go fast enough to push the bullet into the air. So steam was not to be used. One afternoon late in the day, he heard the sound of a mantle clock keeping time. It had been there ten years and had successfully marked off the twenty four hour days. He stood before the clock on the mantle on a red brick fireplace. He took it down and put in the center of his office desk on a paper and leather blotter. He turned it around slowly eyeing it over carefully with a distant look in his eyes. He watched the hands slowly move for an hour and a half. He looked at the wooden oak case. It had a hinged brass bezel ring and a glass crystal over its numbered face. There were two key holes on the front to wind with a winding key the chimes and the main spring. He returned to the mantle and found the brass key there to one side where the clock had stood before. He sat again at his desk with the winding key in his hand. He idly looked at the brass key daydreaming. He turned the clock so that the rear was near to him. He released a brass hasp and undid a wooden service door that turned easily on its two small hinges. He eyed the works inside. There was a shiny brass frame, two steel springs, and a number of gears set on axles that pivoted on bearing pits drilled at strategic locations on the inside of the frame. Yes, there were jewels here to make the motion more frictionless. Ratchets on a mainspring released stored energy in wound springs that springs powered gears that turned the clock hands to tick off accurate time. The clock guided man's activities throughout the day. This was a practical machine. It had however no motion. The hands turned but the clock did not move. Steam trains turned levers, valves, linkages, and wheels to go over distances carrying people and cargo. Still there was a similarity between the clock and a steam train.

Mr. Whittaker for several days studied his mantle clock. It had intrigued him. Yes, he had looked at other clocks and watches before. His thoughts on them before were similar. The workings and motion were interesting. For three days he just looked at the clock. He took breaks and sat in a soft chair over by the window smoking a cigar or a pipe. Some times he had snuff. He looked out the window at the day, activity, weather, nature, and the changing conditions up in the sky. Possibly here in that clock of his was the solution to a new machine of transportation. He could change some things in the clock and get a new engine. Maybe! He got some paper and pencils, pens, ink, and drafting instruments. He drew the frame, the gears, the axles, the journal bearings, the springs, the escapement ratchet and the main springs that changed direction. It controlled the motion of the main train of geared wheelworks. The escapement allowed the energy of the spring power source to be delivered to the pendulum and weights or a balance wheel in watches by a series of impulses allowing a gear tooth to advance or escape from a pallet at regular intervals. A ratchet allowed the spring's energy to be released (escape) to the mechanism of the pendulum or balance wheel. He looked at screws that held the frame together. He examined the pendulum and its motion and the machinery that it worked upon. He drew new arrangements of the parts in changed relationships that no longer were actually a clock. He bought four pocket watches and a grandfather clock. In his office he carefully examined these. A pair of gears turned on one another in opposite ways. Large diameter gears moved faster than smaller ones. Gear teeth had to be twelve to sixteen teeth touching for the angular torque power to be transferred efficiently. The balance wheel turned in opposite directions. It spilled out the stored energy of the mainspring to the clock's movement. A ratchet regulated its action and stabilized the motion of the mechanism. All the shafts, the gears, and the clock arms ran off of this action. The hand wound mainspring was the sole source of energy for the clock. No chemicals or burning hot fire was used. Steam energy burned coal, created smoke and ash, and was potentially dangerous. No body of water was needed to spill water over a mill wheel to turn shafts and axles to create mechanical motion. No animals were used either. Horses required feed, veterinary care, water, and needed periodic rests. Spring steel was a special kind of metal which had the correct necessary properties. Springs may be in a ribbon, coil, or torsional arrangement to work properly. Chester Whittaker seemed infinitely fascinated by these rotary motion machines. Here was a small machine made up of carefully built parts that fit well together in a small space. It worked perfectly well. True it had little power or strength. Redesigning it would change this fault for another application. Possibly it could be rebuilt as a human transportation machine. He wondered for a while if he could build a larger revised version that allowed adequate transportation possibilities for man.

For about two and a half weeks he drew clock parts. Then he stopped. There was a small pile of papers to the upper right of where the clock was placed. All of the thirty five pages he had had drawing on them. He stopped drawing. His mind was full of images of the clock's mechanical components. Chester said to himself, "You can not have motion without time. You can not have time without motion. Maybe they are the same thing. Maybe not." Chester thought of other machines, tools, and steel items that he was familiar with. He thought of guns and cannons. He liked firearms. Nothing useful entered his mind in a new relationship towards his objective of a new machine for transportation. Still he kept working ideas over in his mind. One morning he sat in his chair by the window. He saw a steel bridge that spanned a wide river. The teeth of a gear were straightened into a single rail that passed over the top of the bridge. The idea seemed strange to him. But it lingered. His mind made two toothed tracks and then three. The gear teeth were turned upwards. He changed this to two toothed tracks that had the teeth on their bottom. He imagined a six wheeled car resting on the rail top. His inventor's trance glowed onward. The car had to be powered by springs and gears to use the mantle clock mechanism. Steam, manpower, leverage, linkages, horse or animal power could also be used. How could he set up a machine to use the clock machine to make the car move successfully?

Chester ate a snack of angel food cake, tea cookies, tea, cream, and sugar. Again he idly looked out his office room window at the day's activity and the weather. It was starting to rain. The drops hit the glass panes leaving streaks of moisture. This relaxed him. Chester closed his eyes to rest them and his brain. He took a brief nap.

Upon waking about ten minutes later he saw more of his new car invention. He could build a small test model operating rail cart that could hold about a hundred pounds. It could be made of steel, brass, and copper. Five main springs would power it. A key would wind each one. As one spring wound down, it would trigger the next to operate. About five miles of rail would be covered. A main drive shaft of steel would have the five main springs and a large brass driver spur gear. It would turn two steel axles by revolving a brass pinion gear on each. The axles would spin two pairs of wheels along the rail. All shafts had brass-copper journal bearings. As his mind focused on this idea, he drew it on paper. His mind went onto other developments. He could put a series of gears under the track. Springs world power them. Winding keys would turn the springs to compress them. A ratchet mechanism would control the release of potential spring energy into angular motion on the gear's axles to rotate the gears. The gear's teeth would catch on the bottom of the car on gears on the car's wheels to make it move forward. A series of gears along the track would be positioned. They would all have mainsprings wound by "clock" keys. As the car moved larger gears with larger mainsprings would be encountered. The car would thus be sped up. Acceleration could be achieved! This was part of his first idea objective. A machine that had speed increase capability. Yes, he was creating something new that he had intended to weeks ago at his very first thoughts! On each carriage cart wheel was a flange that rode on a rail. Another flange on this wheel was geared. The spring turned driving gears along the track meshed with it and imparted motion to move it along the rail. The carriage cart had four wheels on each side. On the carriage cart bottom center was a straight rack. This was as flat line of gear teeth. Additional spring turned driving gears pushed it along. A front mounted bar on the carriage cart tripped a ratchet-lock-coil spring assembly. The gear axles were in frame slots. Perfectly sized spring constant mathematics fitted coiled springs that moved the gear axles to engage and power the carriage cart as it came along the rails. At every mile along a track he would put a marble stone column milepost. It would be triggered when the car passed to strike a bell and drop a colored flag that had the number of the mile just passed on it. Possibly five, ten, fifteen, or twenty miles of test track would have to be built at first. He could use a part of his carriage factory to build the car. He owned plenty of land for building the track. The idea of the steel bridge was not really useful. It would be simpler to lay the track over dry land. He made some new drawings of all of this. Again he sat at his desk and handled the mantle clock. The metal, its purpose, and action had a beauty to it. He glowed with enjoyment at the successful advances he made in his thinking. He was after all a very practical, dollars and cents man. He knew profit and labor figures used in all his enterprises were necessary to bring success in anything he set up to do. A new pile of about forty drawings grew to sit beside the first ones he had earlier made of the clock.

Chester's mind, eyes, and body got tired and stiff from his work process. He stood up from his desk, stretched, and took a slow deep breath. He walked over to his soft chair by the window. He looked outside through the glass. The bare tree branches framed the sky beyond. Somehow this sight soothed him. He sat in the chair. He stirred about until he comfortably settled down into it. For over thirty minutes he rested. His mind went from subject to subject in a disorderly way. He let himself slowly calm down.

Chester over a period of weeks bought twenty new clocks, took these apart, examined all the parts, counted the axles and gears, drew them carefully, examined gears circumferences, diameters, width, and the materials that they were made from. There were axis axles, bearing pivots, and jewels. He observed the number of teeth, the teeth heights, basal widths, and shapes. They had involute and hypoid shapes. Some were bevel gears. He inspected the depth and height of the teeth, how they intermeshed, interlocked, and the necessary clearances to move properly. He considered the required lubrication from oil and grease to make them run smoothly. Each gear had a unique pitch diameter. He wanted to experiment with new gear teeth shapes, multiple gear trains, some new better bearings, and better movement springs. The temper of a metal was influenced for how fast it was cooled when heated. This controlled grain structure, toughness, hardness, and strength. He wanted to experiment with this so springs and gears worked correctly, were durable, and tough. Compound springs were used at the start of the rails to get the carriage moving. Springs were put side by side for more turning and pulling strength.

Yes, somehow this ordinary clock had become suddenly very interesting. Some new application of part of its components may be made. A new useful powerful machine may be created. Mechanical motion gave time. Time is the fourth dimension. Space was constructed from the other three. Ordinary man had to travel. Travel was necessary for all of us. Man covered distance. This took time. He could choose any direction and speed. His body on a horse or in a wheeled vehicle were all machines. It always took time to pass over a distance. A clock gave time. It was a machine. Time gave distance when motion was achieved. Maybe a clock like machine could mark off distance as well as time. Time and distance maybe were related. Or could they be just the same thing? This was not obvious. It may be true. There was a subtle similarity between a clock and a horse and a wagon. Both had wheels. Both had stored energy used to pay out mechanical motion. Both were controlled devices with a set speed and direction. As a wagon wheel moved the top counter clockwise to the left, the wagon moved forward and the ground went to the right behind. Two clock gears rolled on each other. The top one moved counter clockwise to the left. The one on the bottom rotated in the opposite direction clockwise to the right. A balanced equilibrium gave both a harmony of purpose resulting from the way that they were built. A spoked wagon wheel usually had a steel rim. They turned on the ground. Somehow this was like a clock's gears. A wheel went forward and carried the wagon and its contents forward in the chosen direction as time elapsed. A clock's gears moved hour and minute hands in a clockwise circular direction passing marked hour milestones. The clock could be built to turn a counterclockwise direction. The clocks arms had an angular motion. Both had circular moving parts that gave out a form of motion. Friction was involved in this motion. The energy of a clock's mainspring could be changed into horsepower terms. This was just basic mathematics. Take a straight piece of spring steel and bend it downward in an arc. It was elastic. The top side would be stretched in tension. The bottom side was pressed together in compression. Energy was stored here. Release it and it recovered to the original straight shape. Springs may be straight, leafed, coiled, or twisted. So a horse and a clock spring were similar. They look different. Gravity worked on both devices. Chester let the mantle clock run down completely until it stopped. The pendulum was still. The tick tock ing sound was gone. The chimes stopped too. He rewound the chime spring and the mainspring completely with the clock key. About eight turns for both would hold the clock for eight days. Chester repeated this winding, unwinding, and stopping five times as a check on accuracy and repeated performance. He wanted to know the winding requirement and time working period of the clock. The construction, mathematics, materials, machining, physics, and engineering design of a horse and wagon and a mantle clock somehow were related. What remained was to look at both and investigate what changes in machinery could be created to build a new traveling device.

In this way, with this objective, Chester Whittaker kept his eyes and mind active looking for some way to do this. A man's two feet and a horse's four hooves are like gear teeth moving over the ground. A wheel is a circle. It is made up of arcs. The gear was a circle that was also made of arcs. Feet and hooves strike out arcs walking. A pendulum struck out an arc. All pass over a distance over a time. A steam driven locomotive has a piston pushed by steam pressure with its rod covering a linear path. Coupled by linkages, this rod powered circular drive wheels to allow the locomotive to move over the ground on steel rail tracks. Linear motion was changed to circular motion that travels linearly over straight tracks. The steam engine was able to develop substantial pulling power and move at a respectable speed. Maybe somehow a clock mechanism could be readapted to do the same.

Chester spent days thinking about various mechanical components. Drive links, capstans, ship's propellers and oars, sails, weather vanes, mill wheels and works, sleds, wheels and axles, saws, inclined planes, pulleys, belts, chains, cables, bearings, shafts, axles, mandrels, arbors, bell cranks, guns, gears, pistons, levers, tools, hinges, brakes, springs, bolts, screws, valves, and wedges. All were familiar. They could be used separately or together as components of a machine. The bullet was the only thing from the gun that traveled. The gun stayed in the shooter's hand. Maybe a bullet shaped wagon powered by clock gears that were spun by coiled springs would be the device that would work.

Somehow a double action revolver with six shots came into his mind and stayed there. The cylinder holds the cartridges. It was turned by pulling the trigger acting a pawl that spins the cylinder on an axle to move and load the next cartridge in to position to fire and pull the trigger to hit the percussion cap primer to ignite the gunpowder charge that pushes the bullet out of the barrel to send it to the target. This also was a motion machine. It was akin to a clock and a horse and a wagon. It resembled the ship's capstan that raises and lowers the anchor.

Chester thought back about his original idea of a cart passing over a wide river on a steel bridge. The river really was the air. The cart was changed into a bullet vessel. He decided what was to be built was similar to his earliest imaging. The carriage cart traveled over land, air, and water on the steel bridge. Likewise the bullet did this also. Maybe in the future many bullets could fly through the air and land in lakes all over the world. Air travelling could become popular. Eventually he stopped drawing the spring powered gear pushed rail car. He left the desk and spent a few days resting his mind sitting in his soft chair by the window. Refreshments were brought in by his helpers. He consumed them. Seemingly he just looked out the window at the world passing by. The bullet cart power would not be in the cart. It would not have to be built on the cart. The engine's weight and complexity were not a part of the moving cart. The motive force was beside the track. The moving cart could be lighter and very simple. The cart and the horse were separated. The horse's leg muscles propelled the cart by pushing on it from the stationary ground beside of the track. Two gear series could be put on both sides of the cart and track or a third one be put under the track in the center. More power was thus possible.

He kept thinking. He saw a bird drop in the air as gravity pulled it down gliding on still wings. The bird actively pumped its wings to gain altitude and recover from the falling arc to climb up higher in the air. How Chester admired the gracefulness of the bird. It seemed to have an efficient mechanical means to get about. It did not get caught up in the dirt, snow, flood, mud, muck, and obstacles placed on the soils surface. The air was light, cleaner, and an easier medium to travel in. Chester spent time outside watching birds. He went over to the riverbank and watched any fish he saw there in the swirling waters swimming by or occasionally jumping out to glide into the air and land with a splash back in the water. Water and air were fluids. The earth was a solid. Chester wondered if he could readapt his geared wheeled rail cart to travel on water or in the air. The water would in time rust the mechanism to make it impractical.

"Humm", he thought. What about travel in the air. Yes, this would really be new. No one was at that time doing that. So back in his office at his desk, he got out some more clean paper from a desk drawer. He drew the cart again several times. He thought then of a gun and cannon that passed a bullet or cannonball out in the air to fly in an arc through the air. Yes, this was the idea! Maybe these were what he wanted and not the rail cart. He drew several bullets. He then on a new sheet drew a number of cannonballs. How could he change the rail cart into an aircraft? He drew a bullet shaped cart testing on a wheeled frame on two rails powered by spring driven gears set along the track. Yes, this was changing his original design to fly in the air. If he got the car acceleration high enough and elevated the final bit of the track upwards to end and launch the bullet into the air he might get it to fly and travel across a distance.

He saw the bullet large enough for one or two people to be inside sitting in chairs or lying down on a mattress. Food, water, safety belts, a compass, maps, necessary medical equipment, and other items could be included. The mantle clock's metal machinery had an attractive wooden case. The cart and bullet could be made of sturdy oak wood that had a strong iron frame and fasteners. Brass and copper trim would make it ever so much more attractive. Maybe a brass and copper sheet metal covered bullet would be nice as well. The bullet would go up a rail ramp maybe five hundred feet, and then the track would level off. The bullet would fly up in the air at the ramp end and the cart would travel on the level part to slowly stop there. Catch hooks would release the cart from the bullet at this time. What should its shape be? It could be a blunt cylinder like a barrel. The front and or the rear may be curved to let the air pass easier, much like a ball. The ends one or the other or both may be shaped more like a bullet or more sloped like an arrow. Would a bird, a fish, a needle or an egg shape be appropriate? It had to pass through the air and stay aimed forward. No other large people carrying object had ever been launched so high for so long through the air. Some more thought and work must be spent on the correct shape to use.

Where would a good place be to launch the "gear driven bullet train"? He looked at maps of England. Country areas have less people. No one would be hurt by a flying bullet in farm areas compared to cities with people, buildings, and much congestion. He looked at lakes, river, hills, and valleys for a suitable track site. He had about a dozen or so marked out. Still none seemed exactly positively suitable. He looked at maps of Scotland, Ireland, and Wales. He wrote notes of several possibilities. He looked at the North Sea and the English Channel. What about a track on pontoons out at sea? It was his original steel bridge idea coming back to him again. Then what he was looking for just hit him. Why not line the track up to launch the bullet over the English Channel and land it in Europe in France, Spain, Germany, or Switzerland in a large lake? The bullet could be made to float. Landing on water would be gentler and cause less destruction than on the land. He could put several round windows on the front of the bullet for the people passengers to look out of. In kind these would be like portholes on a seagoing ship. Amber colored glass was used to protect the passenger's eyes from what might be a too bright of a sun at the flying heights. There was fitted a telescope on a swivel mount so it could be used to look at the sky or the ground below. A barometer was used to tell the height that the bullet was flying at. A compass was also installed to roughly tell the direction the craft was traveling in.

Yes, these were all excellent ideas. He would build a small working model of the device to get the mathematics, mechanisms, manufacturing, and metallurgy worked out. A third of the way up both sides of the bullet's hull was a three inch white band with a small black stripe along the middle of it. A small black bullet was painted at the front of the line near the nose of the bullet. The words "The Airline Bullet" were painted in the center of the side of the craft in black letters trimmed at the edges in gold. He would put on the bullet's metalwork decorative painting with white, red, black, gold, and silver pen lines and scrolling. Then later a full scale version could be built and tested. Land could be leased, borrowed, or bought to set it up on. He could get permission in Europe to "fly" over and land in a lake. He would look over the parabolic equations of projectile motion to get the mathematics fleshed out. He would talk to his draftsmen, engineers, supervisors, and factory workers about the feasibility of his clock motor powered bullet train air craft. Moveable fin vanes and bullet surface could steer it. Later it was decided that two carts were necessary. One was to be very strong to hold and carry the heavy oak and steel bullet. Another cart was behind the first one. It was a motor cart. It carried the large spring motor that pushed the bullet cart along the track and launched the bullet.

The launching track would be located at southeastern England. They located a long wide inland lake there that would do well as a landing site for the bullet. Chester was thinking that maybe he would call it "The Air Line Transport Flying Service." The launching track could be named "The Skyway."

Travel was an interesting phenomenon. It at the same time was like birth and death. You went to new places and met people you may not know. The place you were at was now gone. No longer were you there. Also the people you were with there are gone. Death! Your surroundings, people, and opportunities had changed. Birth! So you explored. Travel broadened your experiences. You learned of new facts and relationships. The new place you find yourself at had new geometries. You had to use time to have motion to go to the new place as you leave the old one. Motion was change. As you moved, the position you are at then was changing.

You were not still. Your body moved over the earth in the air. This was angelic like flight. Some method of moving transported you. You underwent space and time transport. Where you were was lost. Completely lost. You could remember it, but you were no longer there. You saw the world move past you as you traveled. It was mostly solid made up of solid objects. As you moved you saw them move behind you. Where finally you stop was the location that you became a part of. You at that very time of arrival were possessed by a new place. It surrounded you. You depended on it to live. You belonged there and not to where you came from. The food that you ate, the air you breathed, the land you stood on and walk over was new. The place you sleep at was different. The place where your bed was located at night was not the same as before. The light in the sky was some how new. Mostly there were new "local" people at the place you have traveled to. Your actions and conversations were new. The objectives and pleasures you have there were not the same as before you traveled. Yes, travel changed you. Usually this was good. It refreshed the staleness in you. You seemed invigorated. Travel had vitalized you. It had done you good. At first you were the same person in a different place. This different place eventually changed you into a different person. It gave you a new life. The one that you had before had you stayed where you came from, you would have never changed. Had you stayed where you were the new life you would have had after traveling, you would have never had. Travel made your life grow. It strengthened the human spirit. You got new sensations. You sensed the different surroundings and reacted to them to handle the daily tasks at hand. Travel modified your being. It gave the same you different experiences to respond to. And so you were changed. It was a kind of magical spell. Travel was purely a change. It gave you complete freedom. And this can be powerful.

A clock motor was a miracle. It was a finely made machine that worked perfectly well. There were gear clicks with every passing second. The balance wheel fluttered like a hummingbird. Precision made parts worked in harmony to accurately count off the seconds. A clock was a meticulous mechanical symphony performing the inner workings of eternal time, itself. The clock at the launch site had a dial with twelve black Roman numerals.

All of us had our fascinations. Some of these became obsessions. Such things as fame, recognition, adoration, success, religion, romance, wealth, power over people, travel, and artistic expression were likely to cause this in some of us. Chester was controlled by this clock vehicle idea of his. He took a mantle clock and a pocket watch outside one day on a small walk about. He walked about looking at things he saw as he went. He came to a roadway where people, horses, and vehicles were moving along. He watched the traffic closely. He looked at the two time pieces. Another day he visited a railroad station with a train yard, a water tower, a coaling station, a turntable, roundhouse, warehouses, a freight depot, and a passenger station. He had the mantle clock and the pocket watch with him. He watched the starting up, slowing down, stopping, and moving trains. He looked at the machinery and at his two timepieces. He was observing it all hoping for a new insight on his clock vehicle project. He observed the steam exhaust in a fast billowing cloud from the locomotive's cylinder chest. Enormous energy was used to move a large and very heavy railroad train. The piston rod slid horizontally back and forth spinning the driver wheels along the track. The front wheel was coupled by a linkage bar to the rear ones. The large wheels were spoked with hubs at one axle and rims with flanges that held it aimed straight forward on the rails. The turning wheels pulled the train forward on the two steel rails. The motion was rhythmical like a heart beat, breathing, walking, a musical drum beat, and a clock's pendulum arm and bob. The wheels resembled gears without any teeth. Instead they had a running surface that sat smoothly on the iron rails. From the smallest slug and ant to the largest draft horse and elephant, all the creatures that live on the earth have to move about on the ground. Their lives require this. Man and beast are bone, muscle, skin, nerves, blood, fat, lymph, organs, and connective tissue. Wagons, locomotives, cars, and clocks were wood and steel.

Back in his office, Chester looked at all of his clocks. Behind the clock glass a shiny brass pendulum disk bob moved back and forth on the end of an oak arm making soft tick tock sounds that drummed out seconds in the otherwise completely still and quiet air in the large office room. Again he sat in his chair by the window and looked at the traffic passing by in the street outside. He thought to himself. The human being and horses legs pivoted on a hip or shoulder joint to swing an arc when walking. The legs moved forward and reverse as walking occurs. This was like a clock's pendulum swinging forward and reverse in arcs to let the clock mark out time. This resembled a clock's gears moving in a circle or a part of one in a gear train to expel stored spring energy to turn the hour and the minute hands in the twelve hour circle that must be passed twice in a twenty-four hour day. So our legs were like pendulums and gears. One walked. The other measured time. There was a similarity in motion and time. They could be the same entity. The motions of the mechanical components were alike. Both legs and feet and clock arms moved in arcs to attain motion. Maybe legs could be used to accurately give time. Maybe clocks could be used to give motion to travel distances. Everything came and went here and there.

You can stay in one place. This was perfectly alright. Your life seemed secure. The sun will rise, move about in the sky, and set always in about the same place. The objects there mostly were the same. There were always familiar buildings. They had a geometry and a way that they were placed on the earth. You learned where they are. You got used to how you must go to or past them as your needs are. Natural features were present in the world. These may be bodies of water, valleys, rising land as hills or mountains, rocks, and forests. Man did not create or place these. You learned where these are. They were a part of your life. People, plants, and animals were always there. You were also aware of them. Your daily and yearly routine became set. This was due to your abilities, needs, opportunities, responsibilities, and the things that were nearly about you. Now if you changed the place that you were living at, that is, go some distance in any direction that you may choose. Then you have traveled. Motion to do this had occurred. This took time. Then when you arrived at the new stopping place, all was new and different. You are refreshed. The things that you do had changed. You were in a different part of the world. This does have an influence upon you. Most of the time, this enhanced, recreated, and stimulated your life.

Duty and humanity demand that man make progress to better his lot in this world that we live in.

They did many experiments on clock keys, springs, gears, bearings, gear trains, and axles for about a year and a half. There were at first dreams. These became ideas written down on paper. After some talk and planning, they became projects at hand that were carried forward until completion. Some were successful. Others were not.

The watch key had two parts. There were wings of metal that bulged out from the shaft. These allowed the fingers of a person's hand to grip them. They were wide enough from the shaft that it was relatively easy for the hand and wrist to twist the key to tighten a clock's chime and main springs. This was the external energy source of the clock. The shaft connected the wings to the spring axle that turned to twist the spring end to tighten it. The outer end of the spring was mounted fixed to the clock's case. It can not move. The inner end of the spring band was fastened to the side of the spring shaft. Usually it slipped into a slot that held it fast to the shaft. The shaft was moveable as bearings held it in one place but allowed it to rotate about one axis. The shaft had one end that protrudes out of the clock's face. Usually there was fit a slightly smaller square part that let the hollowed out part end of the key slip over it. Turning the key turned the spring's winding shaft and tightened the spring. The spring unwound after about eight days. Rewinding it tightening the spring gave the clock the energy needed to keep its motor running. Some clocks had weights suspended on chains that pull down on gears to provide the mechanical energy to run the clock. Periodically, say once a week, someone must pull on the chain ends opposite the weights to wind the clock. Chester changed the winding key wings so that two human hands could turn a larger version of a clock key to wind up the spring driven rail vehicle. A larger spring was needed to power the carriage-cart on the railroad track. An assembly reduction gear train force transfer was used to make winding easier. Now a strong man could put his back into winding up the rail springs. After many attempts, men found this labor too fatiguing. Later a steam engine was built that spun a large chain that wound the spring motor on the cart that pushed the bullet cart along the track.

A spring was made from steel. Steel may be cast, forged, and machined into any shape. In steam engines, locomotives, and wagon wheel rims steel was made to have the correct shape and power to give motion for efficient and successful transportation. Why could not a steel spring be made to do this too? It could be strong and store plenty of energy when wound up tightly. If connected to ratchets, gears, a case, and wheels, it could give motion for travel. It was but steel like locomotives or wagon wheel rims. A spring was first a long flat steel ribbon. As it was straight, no forces acted on it. It was powerless to do any work. The material in it had stiffness to hold it straight. Being elastic it may also be bent. A wound spring got tension which was a pulling apart of its material. As the spring metal bent, tension or stretching was on the outside surface. The bending spirally twisted spring had an inside surface. The material here was pushed together or compressed. Tension and compression exerted forces to straighten the spring. These forces were used to turn gears and clock arms in a rhythmical matter that produced accurate time keeping. This was how a clock spring functions. Wind up a loose main spring. It became coiled tighter. It wanted to unwind to become looser and was practically used to release its energy as mechanical motion. Many things worked like this. If you pushed on something, it pushed back to resist being pushed on. Springs might be able to provide motion for human transportation.

The earth's surface usually did not move. It was large and had a lot of stationary material in it. Living creatures had to move about upon its surface. Most of them just walked. Man made different ways to do this that are easier, faster, and cleaner.

Chester liked to gaze out of the windows into the sunlight of the day. In the distance was blue sky with clouds moving along. The clouds were puffy white with dark gray bottoms. Trees and buildings were in the foreground. He looked idly among the tree trunks and the branches to watch the distant air far beyond. He got a sense of the extreme magnitude of space. He sensed the possibility to develop new travelling devices to pass here and there in that space. The idea of a clock motor powered vehicle was startlingly exciting. No one had ever built such a craft! The leaves of the trees were all gone. The sky was framed by the wooden tree skeletons. The winter air was cold, dense, and dry. This scene was spiritually hypnotic to him for some reason.

Chester had in his possession a few select clocks and watches. He figured these were alright but having some more of them would let him learn much more about clocks. So for months he traveled to several different cities looking and shopping for many more of them. Soon he had filled his office with new ones that seemed interesting to him. The room was beginning to get too cluttered with them. He found an empty warehouse room at one of his nearby factories. Chester bought some roomy tables and had them set up in this large factory room. He had the clock collection moved there. He had over a thousand of them. For a long time he personally examined each one of them, writing notes in a notebook. Chester hired some draftsmen who used to work for a railroad company. They disassembled clocks and watches and drew them on paper with technical accuracy.

Chester sat in the warehouse room one evening examining his collection of clocks. He looked at one thing and then another. There was an anniversary clock. It was different. It was covered with a glass globe bell jar. It had the usual dial face and works in a frame held up in the jar by four shiny brass posts. There was a rotating four ball pendulum on the base at the bottom. It worked a torsion wire bending it one way and then the other. The clock principle was the same but the mechanism was different. It looked like a jewel in the sunlight. It possessed a charm all its own. It came to him that many of the best clocks he had were made in Germany and Switzerland. The design, materials, machining, assembly, and workability of these seemed much superior to all of the rest. He thought that he might travel to Europe and visit these two lands. He could go to clock companies there, meet the people, look over their clocks and watches for sale, and take tours of their factories. Time passed. He was busy with his work schedule and some at home family matters. He set a date for his European visit and made the necessary preparations to go.

The day came and Chester took the train to Dover, sailed across the English Channel, landed in Calais, hired a horse coach, and traveled across France. He stayed in several inns and ate at fine French restaurants. The French have a flair for very good food and drink.

At last, Chester arrived at the German border. He was graciously allowed to enter the country. In time he came to Essen. This was a large manufacturing center of the land. It was a sturdily built city made mostly of stone. Many streets were cobblestones. Chester stayed at a city hotel and ate at a restaurant that had a bar. He enjoyed the beer they served to him there. Germany made the world's best beer. Chester visited several local clock shops, spoke to the owners, and he bought an assortment of small clocks and watches. He found a coo coo clock made to look like a charming country mountain chalet with squirrels and pine cones on the case and a small yellow bird that came out of a small door to tell the hour. The storekeepers were able to tell him where the best timepieces were made in that area. So taking their friendly advice, Chester visited five factories there. He saw how things were done. He learned much by just looking and talking to the factory people. He hired five German clock makers to return to England for a time to work with him on the bullet.

Next he hired an overland coach to Switzerland. The Swiss were world known for creation of elegant timepieces. He did pretty much the same thing there. He ended up in Geneva. That area had a fresh alpine atmosphere with tall snow capped mountains, scenic green valleys, and deep blue crystal lakes. All was clean and crystal clear. The air was refreshing. Chester ate Swiss cheese and chocolates. Switzerland was famous for these. He found a wooden Swiss music box in a store that fascinated him. He liked the pleasing melody. A brass key outside turned a shaft that wound a spring. Turning a latch, the spring was released to spin a shaft that turned a series of gears. At the end of the gearing was an axle to a brass drum that had bumps on its curved surface. The turning drum rotated. There was a small harp of ten ribbons of steel. Each was of a different length. At the brass drum spun about, its bumps plucked the ends of the harp. This played a familiar melody. Chester bought it and took it back home with him. He hired six experienced Swiss watchmakers to go back with him to England to help him work on his bullet project. Now he had eleven expert European craftsmen to assist him with his clock spring powered flying vehicle. Chester thought to himself quietly on the trip back home of all he had seen and done and about all of the fine people that he had met. Man was always looking for something. He wants something new. Bigger. Better. Nicer. Improvements. More experience. Yes, mankind wants progress!

Large steam locomotives burned coal as fuel to heat steam to power pistons that turned driving wheels which sent the train moving along steel railed tracks. People ate all kinds of food. Horses eat hay. Clock motors had no need of any kind of fuel or food. Clocks only used a spring that was wound tight by a key turned by human fingers. So they were in that respect simpler. Much simpler.

Chester thought on, "A clock. A clock. Yes, a clock. Maybe it was like a clock. It held time. Maybe it also held motion. What else was in a clock? Once upon a time. Yes, that was true. Time comes. It is. Then it became lost in the past. Like a ghost it was almost spiritual. This was like walking on a path out of doors. You go forward. New things passed in front of you. Present things were beside you. Behind you things were gone, lost in the past. Time that is, is suddenly gone. You can not go back to it ever again. Lost time was never again regained. It was one time. Once upon a time." Chester thought on mulling upon this subject to himself. "People, horses, and trains were like clocks. At creation they were wound up. They ran well. Their time went along. They wore out. Their time was gone. All was wound down. They passed out of time and existence. They had lost all of their energy. The matter that was in their bodies left that form to go elsewhere in the world. Everything that was, was some kind of a machine."

Chester walked in contemplation in the English countryside in the warm sunshine.

Chester went to a bank to withdraw money to finance the bullet. He paid a Mr. Shuford Henry Thistlethwaite counting out every bill slowly. Mr. Thistlethwaite was a finance manager for Mr. Whittaker who oversaw a large part of his business concerns. Seeing the money leave his hands, he felt dizzy because he had a falling feeling. Yes, he rightfully owed the man this money. No longer having it on him made him feel sad and poor. Somehow he had a feeling of failure but did not know why. The money would go to build the Airline Bullet. Time will tell if it was really a good investment or not.

Chester went to bed early. He wanted to be rested to give a lot of work to the following day.

Chester had a busy productive life. He had much responsibility. He had an obligation to his wife and family. He had businesses to manage, create a profit, and pay fair wages to his employees. He had a daily routine that kept him occupied. Chester had lived about half of his natural life. Somehow out of all of his time, efforts, resources, and intelligence, it seemed that creation of this new vehicle should be possible. He could make it a reality. Chester could put in the time, work, and money into it to bring it into being. A new device. Maybe the vehicle would work. Maybe he could make some money out of it. Maybe there would be a new, different, and improved way for people to travel. Yes, travel long distances in a short time up in the air. Yes in the sky. Not much lives or stays or travels in the sky. Clouds and birds were all that are ever there. Nothing much else was ever there. Yes, also bats, balloons, bullets, and arrows traveled in the sky. Mostly things stayed on the ground most of the time. Not too very much stayed for any time in the skies above. Was this because they were not supposed to? It was time for people to go to the skies and travel there. He was going to be the man to make this possible. To be able to see something and not to be able to have it could bother someone. To see the possibility of the bullet vehicle and that at the present time it did not exist, bothered Chester Whittaker. He saw men, their lives, and their work like parts of a large clock called creation that lived in time to work to make all that happened happen.

Subconsciously he was possessed with producing the new clock spring powered vehicle. He had daydreams on this that voluntarily came into his mind from nowhere. It took patience, persistence, and hope to create new devices. People and animals crawled, walked, and ran on the ground. This was movement. Clock's arms moved. The clock's mechanical works was called a movement. There ought to be some way of changing a clock machine to produce a motion vehicle that travels so people and cargo could ride in it.

Chester paused for a moment. He went into a daze of thought. He let his mind go along as it would. He thought of how man walked over the earth with his hips wiggling back and forth, two legs going one in front and one in back in turns, and his two feet coming up and down upon the land. Man likewise traveled using horses most commonly.

Riding on a horse's back in a leather saddle, man went where he wanted to. The horse's shoulder and hips wiggled back and forth, its four legs went in pairs forward and to the rear, and four hoofs coming up and down on the ground. Also man rode in buggies and wagons pulled by horses. Steel rims on wooden spoked wheels turned and carried the vehicle along over any desired distance and direction. Metal machinery with steel wheels ran along steel rails powered by hot water in the form of steam carried passengers and cargo over desired distances and directions as the need might be. These three kinds of land travel were both necessary and practical. Man had to have motion to acquire the necessities of his life. It would seem somehow that a simple machine powered by a coiled metal spring turning a properly created gear train could also rotate wheels to carry man and cargo over the earth. This in principle was relatively simple. Just how could it be done? He seemed for the moment to be hypnotized. His mind paused here to see what would come to mind. Chester's reflections continued off in a silky line…...

Chester imagined that he saw a young boy on a small wagon in a city park push on the ground to accelerate and lift a swing to add umph to his ride. This thought Chester was like a pendulum. Time flew. So why couldn't man fly? Man could use clock like machines to travel on the earth and fly. Chester seemed charmed in some type of magical spell by clocks and making a safe useful vehicle out of them. Clock springs could move us about on the earth. Clock springs might be able to move us safely through the air on grand lengthy flights of travel. He would have to work more on this to bring it into being. Man made all kinds of things. Why can't he make this? Yes, Chester wanted this to be. He set his mind to it. He was a man of his own principles and convictions. He had a will power and rules that he lived by. A man ought to be outside in the world doing real things.

It is odd when you were traveling that all the still things on both sides of you seem to move. They really do not move. You were moving. You looked at yourself and you seemed still. But you were not still. You were moving. This seemed magical. The motion of travel was a new thing to your body and senses. You were not standing still upon the ground. You had motion and travel from place to place. Life changed when you traveled. Travel devices were used for recreation, family, military, business, social enrichment, religious journeys, politics, and education.

A man who lived in one place was known to others. If he traveled at first he was an unknown stranger. The people there were also unknown and strange to him. It was the moving that did this. It changed human lives.

You can't be at more than one place at a time. You can travel to another place. You can travel to several places one after another. Where you are, you are. The world has many things in it. Different things. Strange things. Fascinating things. Beautiful things. Travel will let you see some of them.

Man moved best on a plane left and right over the earth's surface. Most of man's motion was inside of or from one to another building. Gravity prohibited him moving up and down. Hills, valleys, mountains, mines, ladders, steps, stairs, a few hot air balloons, and a limited amount of jumping were all he has. Time was the forth dimension. Man was always trapped in the present. He had a past and he goes into the future traveling through the present slowly. He can not move in time. His mind, body, and senses were all stuck in the present. He saw and lived in the time that he saw on any clock or watch. The bullet will gain out travel in altitude and distance. It will be a definite and a dramatic improvement in traveling in these two. It was a large thing to expect a heavy oak bullet with two men in it can travel across two continents from a clock spring launched rail cart on the breath of the wind. But this was what Chester was proposing.

He dared to tame a powerful force in nature. A newly contrived traveling machine would conquer vast stretches over miles of land letting people safely and conveniently move about. He as a businessman would stand to gain in fame, respect, and financially. Gain and loss. Everybody experienced this. It was a part of this real world. What happened to us when this happens? It got hold of our emotions. How do we do this? What does it do to us? The bullet someday will be a gain for the human world.

Chester thought of the human body. It had a framework of bones that muscles moved. A brain and nervous system controlled it. There were sense organs to guide it. The body took in food and water, changed these chemically, and obtained the power needed to do work. Humans could sit still, stand, walk, and run. This was similar to a clock. Both were machines that used energy to move. In a sense both had springs and gears. Human life depended on the heart and lungs where blood and air gained motion. These organs act on compression and expansion. Open and close. In and out. Plus and minus. Sound was also a wave of expansion and compression of the air. The clock spring mechanism acted by the very same principle. So it was alive too. The way a thing was made, that was the way that it shall be. The way things were, mostly they stay that way. Adjacent things acted on one another. Action was always motion.

Life was always moving. Dead lifeless things and objects usually did not move. Life usually had motion. Animals and people moved a lot. Plants mostly do not move. Life was motion. Life had to move. Motion may be simple. Motion can be very complicated. It took the mind controlling the body with its bones, muscles, and nerves to carry out repeated purposeful motions. The mind and the body moved. It was a basic part of their living process. Most of the substance on the earth had no life. It was still most of the time. It mostly existed. Life forms had a purpose and pattern in their lives that required movement to achieve tasks to reach goals. Motion seemed to add a higher quality of existence. Things changed due mostly to motion.

Maybe motion was a more spiritual form of being when compared to the stillness of the nonliving dead objects that stay eternally still. Somehow gravity had us all captured. No one understood fully how gravity was created and operated. This was mysterious. If you traveled, you got somewhere. You may stay there, go back to where you were, or go somewhere else. All three would change you. Travel was an experience.

Objects in buildings stayed mostly still, especially those near the walls. Travel was through doors, hallways, stairs, and steps. Outside most large things were motionless. Land was still. It never moved. Roads and walkways were where most moving was going on. Water in ponds and lakes was still. In streams, rivers, at the beach, and in oceans water moved a lot. Air was still sometimes. Changing moisture, density, and temperatures cause winds that moved the air about. Cities marked the globe. Open country and oceans were between them. Some country was farmed. People must move about on the world for many reasons.

Man's mind usually thought about what he knew or experienced. He had a hard time creating something that he did not know of. He was slow to bring forth the new. He thought that in his mind he traveled. Usually he did not. Most of all human lives were rigid daily routines. Man's mind stayed where it was with old ideas and sensations that he already knew. Man liked to think. He as well loved to talk. He wanted also to travel and have vitalizing experiences. Most people liked to work and buy new things even if they did not need them. All of us liked to see progress, inventions, and new things brought into this world that we lived in. To want things to be better has always been a part of humanity. Man was blessed with the need for hope.

Some things in nature went in straight lines. No, not everything does. But many things did. Fences usually were perfectly straight. They had square corners. Building walls were straight and flat. Halls in buildings were straight. Roads mostly traveled in straight lines. Streams seemed straight but had to sometimes turn to avoid elevation obstacles. The wind blew clouds and smoke in straight lines. Most of the time, if allowed to, people walked in straight lines. The farm work in fields used straight rows. The words in books were printed in straight lines. Fire's flames went straight upwards. Rain drops fell straight downward. Ropes that hang aimed straight down. Seemingly the most successful travel was in straight lines as it wasted less time and distance. The rail track for the bullet and its traveling path in the air probably should be made to go in as straight a path as possible. This would be faster, shorter, and easier to steer it.

There are in this wonderful and beautiful world a great many things that be and many more great things to do. Any new machine or invention was likely to make our globe a little different and better place in which to live. Possible new things would improve our lives, change our habits, and make dull toilsome work easier. If a man took several things and rearranged them into a new combination of parts with a changed function, it did seem likely that we all should advance through this progress. It was the nature of all men to want better things. This gave us hope in our being. Most that is today has been so for a very long time. Few new things if at all come into being. The birth of a new concept, fact, fashion, chemical, musical melody, form of art, law, building, roadway, country, ship on the sea, or machine was indeed rare. All of us will warmly welcome this if it was beneficial. We were sensitive and intelligent creatures. We expected changes. Things as they are stay so. Something changed them. The changes either were for the better or the worse. All that was from then on was never the same again.

Chester cheerfully looked towards the advancement of mankind. He peered out the tall windows of his house and dazed at the sky with the landscape below. These ranging thoughts made him feel fortified and good inside. He became giddy with an inner joy bursting forth from the goodness of his robust spirit. It was as if he was in an emotional communication with the Almighty God, his Maker and Savior. The yellow gold sun beamed down upon the world. All seemed so great and powerful.

Suddenly an odd sad feeling overcame him. It seemed as if the dismal gauze garments of an evil ghost descended upon him. He descended into a depressed mood. He became hazy and faint. Chester looked out at the earth. There was a lot of it. He thought of what might be down there. That was where metals were mined from. Soil had rocks and just dirt. Plant roots went down a few feet. Some animals dug down into it for safe and warm burrows. Mostly the soil was just lifeless. This made him think of being dead and being buried in the earth. Someday he would join it. All in his body would return there. He would no longer be. His end would start him being gone forever. The love and passionate union of his parents brought him into life. He grew up slowly being taught things by people. His body changed and got larger. Eating, breathing, and vital forces that still were not understood gave him life and kept him going. Something caused death to us all. The material that was in our bodies then went into other things. The individual was no more. The earth had the body six or more feet down in the dark still quiet earth where no feeling existed any longer. Chester's eyes became dilated and distant. His skin's complexion lost all color. He took on a haggard look. His pale skin became clammy cold.

He shook his head in grief. He did not like this dratted downhearted mood that had crept upon him. Selecting a paper packet tea bag from a shelf, he put it in a cup. Boiling some water on a stove, he poured it in the teacup. The clear water turned tan then dark brown. Wisps of vapors climbed into the air above the water's surface. Adding some white sugar from a sugar bowl with a spoon, pouring crème from a bottle of crème, Chester stirred this with a spoon. Sipping slowly, he enjoyed the fresh tea flavor. It brightened his mood. From an elaborately decorated cigar box on a table, he selected a cigar, removed the wrapper, cut an end with a small scissors, and moistened it with his lips. Striking a match, he lit the end. After a series of shallow puffs, he had a glowing red ember going that gave him a series of mouthfuls of pleasant cigar smoke. Gray white Smoke curled upwards in the air above his head. The tobacco flavor buzzed his mouth and tongue. This was a most pleasant sensation. Again his mood was elevated and he partially lost the gloomy state he had drifted into. The cigar stimulated him into a contented feeling that lasted a long while. He drank some more hot tea flavored with crème and clover honey. He lit and slowly smoked several more decent cigars. Suddenly his laborious life seemed bright and good once again.

Chester stood up, walked over to the left side of his armchair, and stretched. He was outside of the billowing dusty gray cloud of cigar smoke. The tea, tobacco, and stretching exertion made him lightheaded. His mind wavered dim and then came back to a focus. Looking out the tall windows, he looked about the room.

He walked over to one end of his room where several tall wooden cabinets were. The top halves were glassed so you could see inside. The waist down had drawers. There were his military collections. Each drawer was full of wooden box trays. Each had a lid that lifted up. In them were metal soldiers, horses, wagons, canvas tents, cannons, banner flags on poles, paper mache' hills and mountains, wood and paper trees and hedges, and wooden fences. There were spring loaded cannons that shot steel balls out into the air at a distance of several feet to strike and knocked down soldiers in imaginary games of war. Each piece was well made, brightly painted, and in fine detail. There were forts, castles, knights on foot, and knights on horseback in armor, hussars, fusiliers, grenadiers, cavalry, artillery, officers, enlisted men, British, East Indian, German, French, Roman, and Greek troops. All the imaginable requisites of toy military war action were here. He had an East Indian royal procession such as in an official parade. It had noblemen, footmen, thirty elephants, soldiers, a marching military band, horses and wagons. There were three thousand pieces to it. In the top glass showcases were displayed battalions of armies just waiting to be looked at. They were carefully lined up in marching ranks. There were also a cabinet with cardboard soldiers and items with color printed paper that was glued to the cardboard. Small wooden bases kept each soldier standing upright. A long green carpet was rolled up near a wall. Laying it out on the wood floor, he had a battlefield.

For hours Chester played with these armies. He had to shake that depressed thought that came over him about death. He set up battles between three armies. He set these on the polished wooden floor playing like a child on his hands and knees. He had in another drawer chest a collection of wooden trains with wood track and buildings. He could set up scenic layouts with these too. In still another case he had a collection of sailing warships. There were British, French, and Spanish. He could set up sea battles there as well to provide himself many hours of frolicsome enjoyment. He hummed absentmindedly to himself as he played with the soldiers on the green carpeted battlefield. When playing with the toy soldiers, his eyes grew brighter and a faint color came back to his face. He seemed happy, content, and free from all dreadful worry. The soldiers provided him with adequate recovery from the earlier depressed spell. The sunlight shined through the windows, across the room, and onto the green carpet battle field that held numerous colorful toy soldiers. His firing his cannons and shooting iron balls at his army men caused Chester to think about a flying bullet passenger device powered by clock spring rail car that jumped off a long ramp to fly in the air.

The construction of the bullet caused people everywhere across the land to talk about it. People would say, "Blimey! Have you actually seen the factories where they are building it? Where are these located? Has anyone at all seen the device itself? It is said to travel very fast on the land and then jump up into the air to fly in the sky. It traveled great distances. You suppose it cost a dear fortune to build. No one has ever built such a contraption before quite like this. Do you think it will work? It may not, you know."

Chester in July went to a seaside hotel for a week of business meetings. These were held in a large buffet room. His room looked out over the beach and churning sea. At night, he sat outdoor at a dinner table on a porch under the full moon and stars. Chester drank whiskey. He dreamed up the idea for the bullet flying over the English Channel while looking at the full moon over the ocean.

On a cold winter day he felt a need to get out. He saddled a horse, mounted up, and rode out of town into the English countryside. He came to farm fields where some men with horses and a wagon were gathering hops. He came to ride along a stream. Chester, the rider, sat tall in the saddle and his horse paced along the dirt roadway. They came to a mill pond and a tan rock grain mill. The water wheel was slowly turning changing the falling weight of water on the wheel vanes into rotational motion to turn the millstones that ground grain into fine powder. He rode along a dirt road across miles of empty land and then along miles of woods. Oak trees lined the winding road. A cold whistling north wind blew on the horse and rider. The horse's hooves threw up soil as he pushed forward. Night fell. All was darkness. Soon the moon was rising in the sky.

He came to the bank of a river that after miles of riding came to a large quiet lake. There was a stone bridge where these two met. The trail wound about the lake. He watched the moon in the dark sky. Yellow golden moonlight was upon the ground. It and the sun just hung in the sky. As they passed, in the heavens time on earth marked off. Both seemed to move. Strange but a fresh thought came to him. This was another coupling of time and motion that struck in to Chester Whittaker's mind.

Chester stopped the horse at the bridge to rest a bit before going on. Vapor clouds came out of the horse's nostrils. Chester took several deep breaths of the cool clean night air and relaxed.

On the far side bank of the lake was an inn with rooms. He put his horse in the stable and went to the bar room for food, drink and some friendly local conversation. He drank beer and ate chicken, potatoes, pumpkin pie, fresh bread, a salad, green beans, yellow corn, and a final cup of coffee. There were six men at the table. Mostly they were local farmers who had been talking about fishing for trout in the lake and river. Chester listened with enjoyment. Later the subject turned to grouse hunting in Scotland. Several men told of their luck on trips there to bag some game. Chester listened for about an hour and a half. He grew tired from the long day. He retired to a small room where he slept until morning.

He ate breakfast, saddled and mounted his horse to ride back from where he had come from the day before. The open meadows with livestock on them, ripe farm fields, and forests in winter whose trees were mostly without green leaves gave him natural scenery that invigorated his body and spirit.

Chester with his designing engineer team were accurately estimate the height, path, travel velocity, direction, distance traveled and landing place of the rail bullet.

Chester and his wife, Rosy, at times attended formal affairs that the English upper class held and invited a variety of guests. A Lord Cunningham had a large country estate near Nottingham. It was a dance party at his Manor House. Invited, Chester and wife went. There was a chamber music band, several singers, dancing, banquet food, and speeches concerning business, politics, and religion. There were games inside like cards and outside on the lawn like croquet. A Bishop held Bible reading and prayer. There were rides in a large elegant carriage. Fireworks were exploded at night. Some went on boat rides on a nearby lake.

It does not matter what a man does, he had to put energy in it or it will not be done.

When about in crowds of people that were new to him, Chester would utter, "I would love to meet you." Chester liked to meet new people, to learn new things, and to see new sights.

Chester first built a small model cart powered by clock parts that ran on the ground on wood and steel wheels powered by gears that turned by the motion of coiled springs wound by a watch key. Later another similar cart was made that ran over two steel rails.

To have a complicated design project fail the first several times was a good thing. This taught how much care and effort must be involved to get all of the problems removed to allow the machine to become a complete success. The design objective directed the design, construction, and operation of the device in a certain direction. Certain criteria and constraints were applied to reach this goal. Specifications narrowed the process to aim better at the end target. Repetition was needed to eliminate errors until an operable end was obtained. Diligence was required to see the errors and correct them properly.

A flywheel was considered as useable in the making of a clock powered vehicle. They stored rotating energy. A metal flywheel was a simple disc attached to a shaft of axle that some power source twisted. It was fixed to the shaft with a hub by pins or keys. The hub was made large to hold the shaft and was strung to handle the large forces near the disc center. The main disc was thin and light. At some radius from the axle center there was a heavy rim. The material in the rim had matter and helped to store the rotating energy produced by the power source. The turning was more uniform, stable, and efficient when flywheels were used. Less energy was wasted. A flywheel was put on each axle of the carriage cart to help conserve rotational momentum.

They put flywheels on carriage cart axles. They did not work properly. They slowed it down. After much experimentation they gave this up. As the vehicle never stopped or had to slow down brakes were not put on it. It did not turn so steering was not needed.

Brass rungs acted as steps for the passengers to climb into the bullet hatchway. Ebony, rosewood, mahogany woods were used to create the bullet interior. Red velvet was used to make curtains and pad the walls. The interior looked like the best passenger car that rail travel of that day had to offer.

The clock mainspring unwound, turning the barrel drive, the escape, which is a wheel through a gear train. The escape wheel moved in one direction until it is stopped by the pallet arm of the pallet and fork.

A clock machine had six parts. (1) the mainspring was the source of energy (2) the gear train transmitted the energy (3) the dial train controlled the movement of its hands (4) the winding and setting mechanism (5) the escapement and the balance wheel unit controlled the release of energy (6) the plates or framework or case that enclosures and protected the mechanism.

If complicated engineering ideas and terms were put in everyday language, then people could understand them. Chester's engineers had years of school training and on the job experience. The concepts and vocabulary used for building machines was an easy everyday thing to them. Their drawings and specifications had to be put in the hands of craftsmen who did not understand the how any why of engineering. So the engineers had to express their ideas in understandable words to these people. Some troublesome concepts that had to be clearly expresses were the following:

Decibels were big sounds, mechanical measurements, and the characteristics of the spring, gear, bullet machine, calculations of the lifting force of the bullet, the cart and bullet's weight, and the pull of gravity on its mass, the energy of the forward motion from the gears turned by the wound springs, the energy of the bullet, the wind resistance estimated, the frictional resistance forces in each cart's wheel, axle bearings, and of each wheel's flange on the steel rails, the speed and acceleration of the bullet, the three parametric equations of motion, the time of the rolling and flying points of travel of the cart and bullet at each place along the journey, the rise angle of the track needed for the bullet to fly a successful flight, the exact landing place and the time in the lake, test with a highly accurate machine the turning force of each spring and gear when turned by the winding key to the correct number of turns.

A screw was an inclined plane turned about a cylinder. It could lift weights, overcome resistance, act as a fastener joining two members, and close a vise. Gears were but a variety of a screw. If gears were trained in different sizes, they apply a mechanical advantage.

Chester played around with different types and shapes of gears. Some had sharp spikes like saw teeth, others had rounded circular teeth, others had rods with round balls on the top .Others had square and rectangular teeth.

Chapter 5. The Work Began

At first the power for the bullet cart to be launched on the ramped track was to be horses and then maybe gunpowder using a large cannon. Horses were not strong or fast enough. Gunpowder was tool dangerous. Then steam power was considered. It had power. That was true. But it was so heavy that a steam engine could not go fast enough to push the bullet into the air. So steam was not to be used.

Over longs months of arduous work, a fancy glass conservatory was built to house the bullet standing on the starting track so people and the bullet were protected from foul weather. Gas lights were used to see well at nighttime. The bullet was housed there. Nearby was a brick factory with a large brick chimney smokestack. This was next to a big river near a lake. The water in these bodies came into the factory.

At first they made the spring and gear assembly too small to move the carriage cart with the bullet resting on it. So they increased the size of this a great deal. The wheels of the cart slipped on the track as there was too much twisting power. So finally they made the spring and gear mechanism tie into a gear line on the track. Two gear lines were on the rails and another was in the center of the track. So slipping and power loss were eliminated. This worked well to start the machine in motion. The subsequent mechanisms had to be built correctly to both continue the motion and gradually accelerate it. This took a lot of redoing until it was correct.

To wind the large springs that powered the railroad cart a factory was built of red brick on a river. The water was channeled inside by pipes. It went to a tank. Then the boiler was filled with the river water. Coal was hauled in the factory on a steam train. Piles of it were in ten large bunkers. Dirty overalled men shoveled coal to fire the boiler. It created steam. Machinery using steam power turned mechanisms that wound the huge spring that powered the bullet cart. The wound spring was hauled on a special track to the glass conservatory where the bullet and its cart were. This was used to launch the Airline Bullet. The factory had many complicated parts. There were steel steam pipes cast iron fittings copper plates, rivets and bolts of iron, lead valves, riveted collars, a weather cock, blow off valves to let excess pressure escape, spinning ball governors, bearings, journal mounts, huge steel frame machinery bases, running flywheels, and pistons pushed by piston and crank rods, hopping beams, petcocks ands stopcocks, heart, steam, hot gases, foggy air, fire boilers, coal chutes and carts, numerous brass gages with black metal indicator needles reading on white dials announcing temperature, pressure, and flow rates, thermometers, valves with adjusting wheels, seven tall brick chimneys that blew out columns of billowing black and gray smoke and soot, coiling glass and copper pipes, sprayers, copper fittings, wrought iron security fences, cranes, derricks, hoists, steel archways, a walking indoor pavilion made from a wrought iron latticework, steel frames, gussets, panels, beams, girders, gussets and braces. Steam traps, valves and spigots, stairways, walkways, catwalks, bridges, bars and rails with colorfully pained and decorated signs to described different parts of this city of machinery. Here and there were large music box machines that ran off the factory steam. Steel drums with spikes plucked brass reeds creating melodies.

There was a short run steam train to take people for short rides. Numerous clocks were there too. They were large and sat on top of eight foot steel posts beside walkways. A four story tall steel disc turned on a mount with steam power running it. It had paint on it that when it turned was lovely to look at. The bullet was made of oak staves, steel hoops, stringers, gussets, and plates. Bolts and rivets held all of this together.

A test run was made to see how it all performed. The bullet did get off of the ground. It traveled about five miles gracefully above the treetops. It landed in soft earth and skidded about a mile and a half burrowing out a shallow trench. There were not any passengers on it. It was considered too dangerous to place riders on it yet. It had to be proven first to be a working craft. The oak bullet was not damaged. This was a good test run. Later another launching exercise landed it in a lake. The water splashed and the bullet floated well. Oak was heavy, strong, and water tight.

Early on the idea was to get plenty of elevation, so they should tunnel through a hole in a tall mountain, build the track there, and so let the bullet fly still higher. After some thought, tunneling in a mountain would cost too much. There also was no conveniently near tall mountain to use anyway. A manmade elevation with fill-in dirt hauled by horses and wagons and compressed by tamping was a better alternative. The rail track would run flat for say six miles then go up at a forty-five degree incline about five hundred feet and then level off to run about another mile. This would be about a seven mile track. The incline would launch the bullet into the air.

Four fins were attached to the outside of the bullet. By hand cranks they were adjustable to aim the craft to steer it when it was airborne. A seat for each passenger (initially there were just two) was adjustable to straighten out into a bed. Both the angle the seat and bed made with the horizontal earth was adjustable by hand cranks. They could be horizontal, vertical, or at any desired angle. Safety straps would hold the man in place securely. A circular door was to one side of the bullet. It was closed by large bolts. The bullet was built on a steel frame covered with a heavy oak body that copper and brass sheets made the final outside skin. A series of glass covered gas lights were on its outside and inside. A tank of gas powered these lights.

The track was covered with a clear canopy tunnel of walls and roof made of glass plates set in a wrought iron frame. This protected the mechanism from weather and prevented rust. A fancy wrought iron fence was built on both sides for a decorative appearance and added safety. Gas lamps ran beside the track so all was seeable in the nighttime.

The railroad track ran along the surface of the ground, went off into the far distance, and disappeared at the horizon. The slick polished top surface of the two rails shined like a mirror in the bright daylight sun.

Chapter 6. The Work Continued and Ended

Numerous teams of skilled factory teams went about building the rail carts, complicated spring motor machinery, the steam engine wind up motor, rail track parts, switch, and the oak and steel bullet craft. The geared rail track had to be built a piece at a time. Teams of work crews surveyed and placed the launching track, the turn off switch, and the incline. The incline had wood posts and beams and cross members. Then teams of horses pulled wagons, hauling fill in dirt, crews of men with shovels placed the dirt on the wood structure. The turn off switch had to be made so the spring motor could escape destruction going up the incline ramp. The two flyer men were tested and trained. They studied maps. Many times they got into the bullet and got used to it, wore their leather suits. The doctors made frequent examinations to be certain that they were in good health.
This all was an army of men that worked long and hard on all the different parts of the Airline Bullet extravaganza. It was a large team effort.

Chapter 7. Celebration

People liked ceremony, pageantry, and celebrations. The Airline Bullet people were no exception to this. It was a basic human need common to all people from all lands.

Breaking the hum drum silence, a steam calliope sounded its shrill music.

A parade with marching bands, a steam calliope, public officials, flags, and clowns decorated the roadways around the launching grounds and factory.

There were steam powered whistling rockets that were fired high up into the sky.

Before they launched the bullet into flight, a large band performed, important leadership individuals of grand authority delivered interesting speeches, fireworks were shot off, and a volley of a hundred cannons were fired.

At the celebration before launch an esteemed Episcopal preacher said a prayer for the flight. Chester Whittaker wore a blue double breasted brass buttoned yachtsman's coat and a top hat.

In those times boxing was a most popular activity. At the celebration they held a boxing match between two factory workers who were skilled at this sport.

Chester liked Queen Victoria. Her picture was in his business office, and home den. He kept a small picture of her in his coat pocket. She had nine children. Her eldest son was Albert Edward. He was the Prince of Wales. Chester knew him and got along well with this man. Chester also knew Benjamin Disraeli and William E. Gladstone who was influential in the Liberal Party. Chester was not a politician. He was a businessman. He never held office but he did vote. He thought highly of the leaders of his land and held all of them in great respect. Knowing some of them was to his advantage.

This was the Victorian era of history. There was a most grand style of machinery that was being produced. Steam engines powered factories. Steam engines ground grain, pumped water out of mines, and powered generators that ran early electric lights. Steam rail and ship vessels were being built that were massive and unlike anything ever created by man. Steam shovels dug the earth. Steam powered saw mills cut log timber into planks for using them in building. Steam traction engines plowed farm fields. Steel bridges were being constructed. Man was using new materials and tapping vast sources of energy to power them. The craftsmanship of all of this was extremely detailed and ornate. That period had many men who were highly skilled craftsmen. Their work probably will never be surpassed. Architecture and clothing were typically Victorian which was fancy and a complicated heavy style.

A design goal was a strong spring that was durable and would last for many windings. The spring was to be wound by a steam engine. The spring engine was behind the bullet cart and pushed this forward. It had to be strong enough to run the cart along the track and lift the bullet up a ramp and into the air. Choo choo trains pulled cars behind them. The spring power cart that moved the bullet cart had to push and not pull it. This was because it had a better mechanical advantage, allowed the spring cart to exit a sidetrack and gave more speed needed to launch the bullet. Good spring metal was sought for. Expert advice said that Swedish steel was a high-quality metal well suited to this purpose. This was the land of the Vikings. Several business trips to Sweden were made to locate a source of this. In the cities of Borlange, Sandviken, and Hagfors adequate quantities were obtained.

Chapter 8. The First Flight

England to England Flight:

The completely finished bullet sat still on its metal and wood cart. The builders added a six foot steel spike to the front end. This was to let the craft fly straighter, steer easier, enhance stability, cut the air better, and act as a lightning rod. This spike made the bullet look strange and dangerous. The spring powered motor was right behind it. These were large contraptions that when first looked upon created an awe inspiring feeling. The Airline Bullet was to fly in the air over England as a first test. A track was built in central Kent. About thirty miles south, the landing was to be made in a large lake. Measurements of distance and directions between the track and the lake were carefully and repeatedly made. The track location, spring motor, and steering instructions to pilot the Bullet were all coordinated for the flight.

The oak bullet sat outdoors. It looked large and odd. There was nothing else anywhere like it. This large, cumbersome, complicated, and heavy device did seem a bit far fetched. How could a strange thing like this fly? Most original contrivances when first thought up and assembled in the general manner of construction were hard to accept as workable. Man has a bit of God in him. Sometimes he could work wonders. Heat from the sun in the growing day evaporated the dew from the night before making waves of foggy steam rise off of its surface. The device looked ominous and strange. It looked as if carried some kind of danger or threat. It was part railroad car, part dissected clock, and part oversized artillery shell. The two riders were volunteers selected from the public chosen to be of good health and spirits. A doctor examined them both carefully. They were Earnest Lloyd Cagle, school teacher of chemistry, and Wriston Thomas Jones, a coal miner. Both signed a legal form assuming complete responsibility for their behavior and accepting the risks of traveling in this unproven device. It could very well be the end of their lives!

These two passengers wore a brown leather suit with copper ankle lets and bracelets. The safety suit for each of the two passengers also had cotton, wool, and felt lining. This was for comfort, and cushioning. The safety suits that were made that were padded with wool to keep them warm. A helmet of leather and copper that covered the entire head was also used. The leather and copper helmets were also lined with wool. The helmet covered and protected the head and face. Holes were there for eyes, nose, and mouth. A pair of goggles covered the eyes. Glass goggles were fitted to the two men to protect their eyes. They were made of black leather, copper, and glass. Oversized black leather boots lined with wool on the inside were made. They were equipped with copper soles, The two men when suited up looked like knights.

A steam engine on a specially built wagon was hauled from the factory by a team of six white Shire draft horses. It was positioned near the spring driven cart engine. Coal was shoveled from the wagon bunker into the boiler. A fire as built and a head of steam pushed gases in the air from escape valves. Soot and smoke left the steam engine smokestack. Several men hooked up a large sturdy chain from the steam engine to a large gear to one side on the bottom of the frame of the spring engine. Over about four hours, the steam engine slowly drove the chain in a loop that wound the spring on the cart spring engine. Ratchets kept the spring axle from unwinding. Coal was shoveled continuously into the steam engine boiler. Steam pushed a piston back and forth. Its rod turned a crankshaft. This rotated the chain connected to the spring engine. The enormous loose steel spring slowly was tightened. A large English china tea pot was set on the top of the boiler. Steam eventually built up in the teapot and the handle whistled. This pot made fresh hot tea for thirty tired workmen. Finally the work was complete. The steam engine shut down. The fire went out. Heat left it. Smoke and soot stopped fuming out its chimney. The horse team hauled the steam engine wagon away from the railroad track, into an arc, and then back in the direction of the brick factory.

The two men walked up a set of steps onto a platform beside the bullet. They each turned around, put on their helmets, waved at a crowd of people who had gathered to watch the launch, and climbed in a doorway to get inside the craft. They closed the door from inside and spun bolts to lock it securely in place. Workmen inspected the spring motor cart and the cart holding the Bullet. After a time, their foreman waved his hand in the air. Chester stood beside the spring, motor cart. He hit a lever on the side of the framework with a hammer. This was a safety lock that blocked the engine. The spring's power was activated and put enormous force on the motor. Axles and gears spun. The two carts started slowly to roll. They sped up. Along the track they went. They went a few miles. The crowd at the launch site eventually lost sight of these vehicles. A forest of trees came up and trees were passed at high speed. The carts got to a horrendous speed. They came to a turnoff Y track. The switch was triggered as soon as the bullet cart had passed the sidetrack. This kept on going forward. The spring cart made a right turn, rode on for a part of a mile, slowed and stopped. The bullet cart was shoved by the spring motor cart in the last seconds of their travel together. This bullet cart accelerated greatly. The track gradually went up hill on the launching incline. At about five hundred feet up, the bullet left the cart and went forth off the ground for the first time in the thin air. The cart went along a level track and due to gravity and friction, slowed to a stop. The bullet climbed rapidly. Vapor streams appeared at the rear of the bullet in the air that it had passed through. This appeared like smoke.

The craft climbed steadily and leveled off. The two me inside peered out the windows at the land below them. It was moving behind them at a rapid rate. They were happy, amazed, scared, worried, and exhilarated by all of this. The lake at last came into view. The controls were manipulated causing the bullet to descend, glide, and splash into the lake. The bullet threw up much water. It spun over many times but went straight ahead. After a time, it slowed and stopped bobbing peacefully in the water. A lovely wooden steam ship came from a shore dock. It reached the bullet and stopped. The ships crew tied three ropes to the hull of the bullet and towed it slowly back to the dock. Returning, the bullet was put in a specially made pier. Ropes were untied from the steam ship. New ropes tied it to the dock. The bullet's door way was opened and the two men came out. People cheered and yelled at what they had just done. Man his flown! A doctor examined the crew and let them go when nothing adverse was found. There was a ceremony with a prayer, words of adulation, and a banquet dinner feasted in a large tent that had been erected close by. All the people there were extremely excited and happy what had just happened. The dangerous voyage had been a complete success!!

The bullet might have military uses too. Possibly it could spy on the enemy, carry supplies, troops, and weapons. A flying bullet craft could have weapons in it like guns or explosives to use in an attack from the air against the enemy.

From England twenty miles inland the bullet was to fly overland, then across the English Channel about twenty-five miles, and finally about thirty miles across inland France to land in a long large lake near a river. Chester made arrangements with the English and French government officials to make this between nations flight. After the flight was over, the bullet was loaded on a specially built horse pulled wagon, then loaded on a special train, loaded on a ship to get it back to England back across the English Channel, then put on another train and carried back to the original launch site for future use. Later Chester wanted to build a train, launching ramp track, factory, in France near the landing lake and river. This would let him fly the bullet in both directions and not just one.

The entire launch track was seven miles in length. They had considered using a steam locomotive to pull or push the bullet cart up the launching ramp. Also they thought of a steam engine that turned a pulley pulling a rope that went up track to a pulley and then back to the bullet cart. This would pull the bullet cart up the launch track. The steam engine was too large, heavy, and slow to work well. The final idea was much different and simpler. The spring motor engine on a cart with wheels was placed behind the bullet cart and pushed it onward. This motor ran on a ground level track. It sped up more as it ran. The two carts and bullet came to an incline in the track. The spring motor cart was triggered by a mechanism in the tract to disconnect and it went on a side track as told to by a rail switch and not up the launching ramp. It was not to go up in the air. For it to do so may damage or break it. The bullet flew in the air. The bullet carrying cart did not fly in the air with the bullet. The bullet cart went on for about a mile on a level track it had reached after climbing the incline. It simply ran until it stopped. The two carts had to be separated. This made the bullet carrying cart lighter and it went up the ramp faster. The spring motor cart was heavy. It was not to go up the incline as its weight would slow the bullet cart down and the bullet would not go fast enough to fly off the bullet cart at the top of the incline. The engineering dynamics of all of this was carefully worked out and tested beforehand. The bullet was steered to land in a large French lake. Hitting the water, it would make a big splash and float safely. A steam boat came out to it and towed it back to a specially built dock. The people left by a hatch. There was to be a celebration Champaign, wine, the best French food, speeches, fireworks, singing, musicians and dancing. A soirée (party).

The Nineteenth century saw advancements in using artillery and predicting the flight of ballistics. They learned to accurately calculate elevation, windage, the powder charge, and all the necessary factors to aim accurately and hit targets over miles of distance. There were three parametric equations of parabolic motion needed to do this. Chester hired five experts at this. His Chester Oates Whittaker whiskey brewery in Glasgow, Scotland made oak vats and whiskey barrels needed to brew, store, and ship that product. He got his craftsmen to build the oak bullet shell and railroad ties out of oak taken from a Scottish forest. In Cardiff, Wales, Chester bought the coal that he needed to power his factories. Gravel ballast was also obtained there to use to hold his rail track and ties down on the roadbed. Wales was a mining area producing raw goods taken from inside the deep earth. Iron at Birmingham plants Chester owned was forged into the rails and other steel parts needed to build the Airline Bullet.

Chapter 9. The Final Big Voyage

Flight England to France:

There was a different spring engine built for the flight to France. It was about the same in size as the earlier one, maybe a little bit larger. It was more powerful. The spring was a triple laminate of steel spring metal. This was needed for the higher and father flight. The bullet and its cart were pulled out of its shed by men using pulleys. They put it on a nearby steam train car that was made especially for the bullet. The steam train carried the spring motor cart too on a separate rail car. A group of coal gondola cars were loaded with coal. They were to power the steam engine that wound up the spring motor. The launch site was at a different location. The track that was used was built anew aiming across the English Channel and into the side belly of the French countryside at a lovely large, deep and long lake landing site. Horses pulling wagons hauled soil to build the mound for the incline. Men with shovels and strong backs piled up the dirt and placed the stone ballast, placed the sturdy oak railroad ties, and set the tracks down straight and firm. This work took months.

The flying machinery arrived at the launch site. It was removed from the train and positioned at the start of the track. The steam engine as loaded with coal, fired up, steam pressure built up, and began to wind the spring motor. This took five hours. There was a speech, band music, a prayer from a local Anglican priest and a toast of wine to the bullet, its makers, and the two flyer men. The two men in their leather suits climbed the wooden stairways to a platform, entered the craft, and carefully closed the door.

Chester Whittaker took the same hammer he used before and hit the bar that let the spring engine start moving. The two carts slowly at first rolled along the track way. Speed built up until the moving device was a blur. The six miles was passed without incident. At the bottom of the ramp incline, the spring motor cart took a side spur rail. The bullet cart sped up, climbed the incline and launched the bullet into the thin blue air. The cart rolled along the level track at the top of the mound, slowed, and eventually stopped. The bullet climbed steadily. It came up to where some clouds were. It leveled off at about 15,000 feet and flew eastwards across England. The two men in the bullet flying across the English Channel looked at the land, sea, sky clouds, and saw out the round windows a flock of ducks flying in the clouds.

Both men were excited but this was a longer more risky flight as it crossed sea water and ventured into a foreign land. They were unconsciously apprehensive. The bullet crossed the countryside and came to the cliffs at the western bank of the English Channel. The water had waves on its surface that were visible from the flying projectile. Soon they were in the middle of the Channel. England was a small line in the distance. The sky was sunny and seeing was easy. The French coast came into view. The beach and farmland was there.

Minutes ticked on by. The bullet flew on across the French landscape. This was a different place. Buildings looked different than what was seen in England. Farms and small villages passed underneath. One village had a pretty large church with a tall fancy steeple. More farms, roads, and villages came and went. A long wide blue body of water appeared up front. The bullet started loosing height. It descended until the trees were not that far away. The lake waters came up and hit the bullet's belly throwing splashing water up at each side to fantastic heights. The bullet slowed and bobbed inn the water. It slid forward and came to a stop. A steam ship was seen in he distance aimed in the bullets direction. It came up beside the bullet. Men on its deck tied three ropes to the bullet's hull. The steam ship turned and had the bullet in two. A wide bow wave grew and stayed there. The steam ship came to a dock. It stopped and let the bullet drift into its specially made pier. Men at the pier untied the bullet from the ship and retied it to its own dock. The two passengers opened the doorway and came outside. The crowd there cheered them. Some one fired a cannon.

The two flyers were checked over by a doctor who found them in good health. They walked to a colorfully decorated pavilion with many colorful flags fluttering in the air. The two men were awarded a couple of blue ribbons by a French government official. In the bullet were gifts for the Frenchmen. These were found and brought out to the pavilion. The French government officials had gifts to give as well. France then was the Third Republic. Its rulers were President Marie Francois Sadi Carnot, and President of the Council Charles Floquet and Pierre Tirad. The British Rulers were Monarch Queen Victoria and Prime Minister Robert Gascoyne-Cecil. They sent ribbons, plaques, swords, and metal badges to exchange as good will gifts. Queen Victoria gave Chester a blue ribbon and a parchment for his labors and success. The ruler of France gave him a gold ribbon, Champaign, and a gold and silver sword. Chester gave the French ruler a barrel of Irish and Scottish whiskey, casks of English beer, fine English china and silverware, a white leather bible, English chocolates and cheeses as a gift.

The bullet shot from England to a lake in France went one way. The bullet would have to be flown on the return trip from France to a lake in England to make the trip a complete journey. For now it was carried back to England by horse team wagons, steam trains and steam ships. Much work was to be done to improve the flying oak and steel bullet, its tracks, carts, spring motors, steam engine wind up machinery, support workers, and ground facilities. The start was made. It was a success.

Chapter 10. Conclusion

It was a damp and cold December day. The wind that blew could cut you in two. Chester Whittaker walked about outside winding himself down from some hours of work in his office. People were walking about. Horses and people on their backs in saddles moved here and there. Horse drawn carriages carried people and packages about on the roadways and streets. Chester came to a wooden gate in a masonry wall. Passing through, he came to a large grassy opened area. A dirt path carried him across it to the more open country. Along a hedgerow he walked into a wood. The trees covered the space overhead. All of the leaves from the preceding fall were all over the ground. The path crossed a stone bridge over a bustling stream. He saw fish and weeds waving back and forth in the clear waters. Walking further the pathway came to a large open plain. There was a line of trees in the distance with a grassy meadow in the foreground. Chester looked out at the tree line. Its branches framed the border to the sky above. In the sky was blue air and white wispy clouds. His mind became rested and came to a thought that he had recently been successful in creating a new way to travel up in the air, free of the earth, and go a long distance. He was happy now to have traveled safely there. This made him contented and proud inside.

Epilogue:

Chester grew older. His wife, Rosemary, at age eighty died of a stroke. He lived to age ninety-five when very old age overcame him. His veins and arteries just no longer worked adequately. His heart stopped on afternoon. Chester went to his Maker. He left ten percent to his church. The rest was willed to his children. He left a fine collection of business assets, cash, stocks, worldly possessions, friends, and accomplishments. His grave was at his father's farm at the edge of a wheat field just beyond the woods. The marble marker said:

CHESTER OATES WHITTAKER

"I HAVE ENJOYED BEING ALIVE ON THIS EARTH. LIFE WAS GOOD TO ME. I MET MANY NICE PEOPLE. IT IS NICE NOW TO BE WITH GOD IN HEAVEN. "

His descendants kept his businesses in good operation. The novel clock spring vehicles were still made but gained improvements. In the year 2040 there was an energy crisis. Petroleum products inflated greatly in cost as to nearly be unaffordable. Spring cars were made for people as a substitute. They used no gasoline. Electric motors efficiently wound the springs. Gearing would give about a hundred miles on a single winding. The Airline Bullet was actually the first of many useful spring powered devices. If a clock could run eight days on a winding, similar machines could do wonderful, amazing, and practical things too. Spring powered boats, airplanes, and trucks were constructed. There was built a spring and gear powered fan that cooled people in the heat of summer. A spring powered food mixer was created. It was small enough to use in the kitchen. They also manufactured spring powered music boxes, clocks, and watches too. No steam, gasoline, horse, or ox was needed. The only necessary requirement was a flexible band of metal that could be made tighter to turn shafts. Turned shafts could do useful things for mankind. Chester's life had not been in vain. Spring power was practical and affordable.

Chester's ancestors in the future in 2060 made spring powered land vehicles. These were economical and successful. Electric motors wound up the springs. They were a good substitute for gasoline to power cars. Gasoline prices had been raised very high.

Chester Whittaker left behind a body of work that was to benefit all future mankind to come.

Ten years after its first flight, the bullet was out of date. Newer versions had been built that were cheaper, smaller, lighter, and more efficient. The original bullet was gathering dust in a large shed. It had been abandoned by time. Some concerned citizens had remembered it. They sought its whereabouts and after some difficulty located it. It was still in custody of its owner, Chester Whittaker. Contacting him, they convinced him to put it in the British Museum. It had an honored place along with clockwork external motors, rails, and statues of Chester and other persons. It in time became a popular exhibit.

The earth was made up of various substances. Mineral, vegetable, animal fire, water, air, earth, electricity, and what have you. Early man made things he needed mostly out of leather, wood and stones, and later metal. He had always made things. Single or teams of craftsmen made items. Later factories manufactured good in large numbers.

The End

<<<<<<<<<<<<<<<<<<<<<<<<<<<<The Airline Bullet>>>>>>>>>>>>>>>>>>>>>>>>>>>>>

www.ingramcontent.com/pod-product-compliance
Lightning Source LLC
Chambersburg PA
CBHW081405160726
48000CB00010B/3478